School for Trophy Wives

by Freyda Thomas

Inspired by Molière's
L'Ecole des Femmes

A SAMUEL FRENCH ACTING EDITION

SAMUEL
FRENCH

FOUNDED 1830

SAMUELFRENCH.COM
SAMUELFRENCH-LONDON.CO.UK

MUSIC USE NOTE

IMPORTANT BILLING AND CREDIT REQUIREMENTS

CHARACTERS

ARNIE (PHIL FORREST) – A Hollywood Producer (50s)

AGNES – Arnie's ward, 17

HAL – A young suitor to Agnes, 20s

CHRIS – Arnie's friend and the voice of reason (50s)

ALÓN (A-LAWN) – A Hispanic, longtime factotum to Arnie, (30s and up)

JORJINA (HOR-HEENA) – Alón's wife, (30s and up)

EVE– Agnes' long lost mother (40s)

RON – Hal's father, a friend of Arnie's (50s)

There is a non speaking role for a male who plays **PIERRE**, (a hair-dresser), a **MASSEUR** and a **SCRIPT READER**. For budget considerations, this character could be eliminated, as he does not appear in the original play and has no lines.

AUTHOR'S NOTES

There are two acts, one scene in Act I and two scenes in Act II. The play runs approximately two hours.

Agnes' name is pronounced AG-ness by everyone but Alón and Jorjina, who pronounce Agnes' name as An-YES.

For student productions, there are a lot of possibilities for "extras": set people seen on stage, prop people, cameras, etc. The director is invited to play with the movie set scenario.

For J.– who knows why.

ACT ONE

Scene One

(Option: Prior to curtain rise, all the actors cross the stage, back and forth, with various movie set props. No dialogue. When everyone clears, the actors playing **ALÓN** *and* **JORJINA,** *enter with clapboards, stand down center and clap them together three times. From offstage we hear "And Action!" The actors exit and the lights come up on...)*

(The patio of a sumptuous home in Bel Air [or Malibu]. [Option: Over the top of the set we might see sound stage equipment, as though a movie was being made.] On the set, the predictable luxury abounds. We are poolside. A patio table and four chairs, a bar, a fridge. Piles of scripts everywhere. Budget permitting, a reader can enter, from time to time throughout the play, deposit a script and pick up another. A fence, stage right, separates **ARNIE**'s *house from his neighbor's. Stage right there is a façade of a balcony with two windows and, under it, the side door of his neighbor's house. In it live three people—temporarily:* **ALÓN** *and* **JORJINA,** **ARNIE**'s *two factota, whose current job is to watch over* **AGNES,** *the strictly brought up young thing* **ARNIE** *plans to marry. Enter* **CHRIS,** **ARNIE**'s *writer/director/friend, just back from location. He looks around, sets down his suitcase and calls out.)*

CHRIS.
Hello? Hello? Is anybody here?
Hey! Where did everybody disappear?

(The door to the neighbor's cottage opens and **ALÓN** *and* **JORJINA** *enter.)*

ALÓN.

¡Holá!

JORJINA.

¡Holá!

CHRIS.

¡Holá!

ALÓN.

It's Señor Chris!

JORJINA.

¡Yo sé!

CHRIS.

What's going on? What did I miss?

ALÓN.

A lot of stuff.

CHRIS.

In two months since I've gone?

JORJINA.

The boss, he's loco.

CHRIS.

Great. What's going on?

ALÓN.

You got to talk to him.

CHRIS.

What can I do?

JORJINA.

You are his friend. He have respect for you.

CHRIS.

So, what's the problem?

ALÓN.

(as **AGNES** *wanders out on the balcony, looking for* **HAL**)

Ella. [Spanish— eya]

CHRIS.

What a sight!

Who's that?

ALÓN & JORJINA.

His fiancée.

CHRIS.

His what!!??

ALÓN.

That's right.

He want to marry her.

CHRIS.

Her!?

JORJINA.

Sí.

CHRIS.

Oy vey.

JORJINA.

And he won't hear a single thing we say.

CHRIS.

What else is new?

JORJINA.

Well, you know him. When he

Gets an idea, there's no boundary

He won't jump over to make it come true.

That's why we called you back.

ALÓN.

Sí. We need you.

JORJINA.

Alón! He's coming! Shh!

(ALÓN *and* JORJINA *run back into the neighbor's house as* CHRIS *puts down his things and goes to the bar to mix drinks.* ARNIE *enters, talking on his cell phone, cigar, sun-glasses, shorts, the whole Hollywood regalia. He sits*

on the lounge chair as he continues his conversation.
CHRIS *points to the bottle,* **ARNIE** *nods to him.)*

ARNIE.
Ron— you old putz!
I have to see you— no ifs, ands or buts!
It's been four years!~ I know. That's much too long.
Where were you all this time? Where!?

(to **CHRIS***)*

In Hong Kong!
How's Hank? Right, Hal. He did? He wants advice?
Of course I will. He's your son.

(to **CHRIS** *who is fixing him a drink)*

Hold the ice.
With open arms... Just send him here to me...
Whenever. So, what else is new? Let's see...
I got a big, new movie deal, my friend.
You want a piece? I guarantee back end!
We'll talk. Lunch at the Ivy. Thursday. *¡Ciao!*
I told you, send him over here right now!

(He hangs up.)

My old friend Ron. His kid's a would-be writer.
He's got a script about a midget fighter.

CHRIS.
Let's change the subject.

ARNIE.
What's the subject?

CHRIS.
You.
This cockamamie thing you want to do.
Get married!?

ARNIE.
Oh, you heard.

CHRIS.

It's true?

ARNIE.

Oh yes.

CHRIS.

No talking over things?

ARNIE.

No.

CHRIS.

I'm to bless

This union?

ARNIE.

Bless. Yes.

CHRIS.

Marriage to a child.

ARNIE.

She's not.

CHRIS.

She is, my friend. You've been beguiled

By you know what.

ARNIE.

What?

CHRIS.

Midlife crisis!

ARNIE.

Not.

CHRIS.

Then you're in love?

ARNIE.

I am.

CHRIS.

And her?

ARNIE.
                    She's got
A very strong affection for me.

CHRIS.
          Ah!
"Dear Uncle Arnie!" This is too bourgeois!
It's so predictable! Lights, camera, action!
Come to the studio— see the attraction.
Quiet on the set! Take one, two, three,
It's Arnie in his latest comedy,
The working title? "Screwup of his life,"
As our poor hero takes a trophy wife.
I thought that you were sworn to bachelorhood.

ARNIE.
I changed my mind.

CHRIS.
          And you're convinced you should?
Why now?

ARNIE.
     Why not?

CHRIS.
          You've ridiculed your friends
For years, you've laughed at tinseltowny trends.
What will they say to you now? Ha! He's gone
And joined the rest of us. They'll carry on
As you have done to them when rumors fly—

ARNIE.
There won't be any rumors.

CHRIS.
          No? And why?
You'll join the ranks of men who just ignore
The writing on the wall. Well, it's a bore
To fret about your wife's activities.
Your wealth can always bring her to her knees.

ARNIE.

Look, Chris, I'm gonna do it, come what may.
I'm fin'ly getting married! You should say
Congratulations, not "you've lost your mind."
I tell you, this girl is a gem— a find.

CHRIS.

They all say that— at first.

ARNIE.

I know they do.
Who's made more fun of them than I? But you
Will take one look at her and understand.

CHRIS.

I've seen her, and you've gone to Disneyland.

ARNIE.

Ha ha. You know I hate the "trophy wife,"
Whose aim is to degrade her husband's life,
Who smiles, cajoles and wiggles, calls him "honey,"
Then grabs a credit card and spends his money.
She flatters, pumps him up, hangs on his arm—

CHRIS.

And he feels young.

ARNIE.

It works just like a charm.

CHRIS.

He's blind—

ARNIE.

Therefore, can't see what will occur
On Wednesday afternoons with her masseur.

CHRIS.

Or Friday mornings with her pers'nal trainer.

ARNIE.

To everybody else it's a no brainer.
And no one says a word— the golden rule.

CHRIS.
Don't ever tell a husband he's a fool.
So you found the solution?

ARNIE.
Don't you see?
Those bimbos make a total mockery
Of men, but this one, well, she's innocent.

CHRIS.
In other words, she's in development!
Where did you find her?

ARNIE.
Fresno.

CHRIS.
Fresno!?

ARNIE.
I
Was shooting up there. It was late July—

CHRIS.
When?

ARNIE.
Thirteen years ago.

CHRIS.
Ah. Tell me more.
(aside to audience)
There may be quite a big surprise in store.

ARNIE.
Her family owned a little raisin farm.

CHRIS.
Girls from the farm do have a certain charm.

ARNIE.
She always did. When she was only four,
She knew just how to make a man adore
Her every word— because she didn't try

To wheedle or manipulate or lie.
The family's poor. They hardly could afford
To clothe and feed her. I made her my ward,
And sent her to a strictly private school,
Where she learned to apply the Golden Rule:
Live simply and obey. Don't ask a question.
Don't ever even offer a suggestion
That things could be accomplished differently—
Say yes and smile. In point of fact, agree.
I didn't want her turning out to be
Like all these other nightmare brats you see.
I'd visit, bring her little things, we'd play,
I thought of her in a…paternal way,
Until it came to graduation day.
I went, of course, to watch my protégée
Walk down the aisle. The aisle! What can I say?
I realized that she might go away,
And then and there I saw my brand new life—
With Agnes, once my ward, and now my wife.

CHRIS.

But marriage is—

ARNIE.

The answer. Look at me.
I have it all, and there's the tragedy.
Without someone to share it, what's it for?
I wanna come home, walk through my front door,
Call "Honey?" hear it echo down the halls—

CHRIS.

(aside)

And see her playing with her Barbie dolls?

ARNIE.

Besides, if I want kids, what better way?

CHRIS.

But Arnie—

ARNIE.

Go on, say what you may say,
She's perfect. She knows nothing. She will thrive
And never even see Rodeo Drive.
I brought her here directly from the school—

CHRIS.

Where she will now turn you into a fool.

ARNIE.

She won't. I told you, she's been so well trained
To be obedient, it's all ingrained
In her. Oh God, the money I have spent
To keep her absolutely innocent.

CHRIS.

Why is the little wonder right next door?

ARNIE.

My neighbor's on location. Furthermore,
Jorjina and Alón watch over her.

CHRIS.

You keep her up there like a prisoner?

ARNIE.

Of course not! But she doesn't know this town,
I can't just have her walking up and down
The streets. She's too naïve. She'd say hello
To Jack the Ripper, Charles Manson! So,
I keep her safe.

CHRIS.

So near and yet so far
From everything.

ARNIE.

Exactly. And you are,
Since you are such a trusted friend, invited

To eat with us tonight.

CHRIS.

(*not*)

I'd be delighted.

ARNIE.

A simple little supper, just we three.
She'll cook! You'll see how very satisfactory
She is.

CHRIS.

I'm confident that I'll agree.
But are you sure you wouldn't rather wed
A girl with sense?

ARNIE.

What good is sense in bed?
Or anywhere? A simple girl will never
Know how to commit a sin—

CHRIS.

How clever.

ARNIE.

So?

CHRIS.

So?

ARNIE.

You'll stay and meet her?

CHRIS.

If you want.
But I must warn you, I'll be very blunt.

ARNIE.

Fine. She won't get it. Sheer simplicity
Describes my fiancée.

CHRIS.

Can't wait to see.

(**ARNIE**'s cell phone rings.)

ARNIE.

Phil Forrest.

CHRIS.

Not again?!

ARNIE.

(Motioning him to be quiet)

Right, baby, right.
We'll get that script sent out to you tonight...
Hold on— the contract's on my desk inside...

(to **CHRIS**)

I'll be right back and you can meet the bride!

(He goes into his house to finish the phone conversation.
ALÓN and **JORJINA** stick their heads from their windows
next door.)

ALÓN.

Señor!

JORJINA.

You fix it?

CHRIS.

Not yet! But a plan
Is brewing. Keep him spinning, if you can,
Distract him.

ALÓN.

See? I told you he'd come through!

JORJINA.

You told me? Very funny—I told you!

(They slam their windows and argue in Spanish as
CHRIS dials his cell phone.)

CHRIS.

Eve? Chris. Get on a plane. No, right away.
I need you here by five o'clock today.

Just trust me. I'll be there to meet you. Great.

    (He hangs up and speaks aside.)

It would appear the horse has left the gate.

    (**ARNIE** *re-enters, finishing his conversation)*

ARNIE.

You'll like the script. It's sharp, it's clean, it's sleek.

Just have your agent call me by next week.

I love ya. Ciao.

    (He hangs up.)

      Ah, Meryl. What a star.

CHRIS.

And who's Phil Forrest?

ARNIE.

    Me.

CHRIS.

    Again?

ARNIE.

    You are

So dense about this business, sometimes. Here,

A name has power. Forrest sounds sincere,

Yet strong.

CHRIS.

    But Arnie—

ARNIE.

    Sounds like a big schmuck.

Phil Forrest is a man who brings good luck

To everyone—especially himself.

CHRIS.

So Arnie's—

ARNIE.

    In the can, on the back shelf.

When I was young, just starting out, ambitious,

I used that name. OK, I'm superstitious.

I guess I wanna be that guy again.

Phil Forrest is a classy gentleman.

CHRIS.

(not buying it)

There's something else. Some other reason.

ARNIE.

What!?

CHRIS.

(after a moment of reflection)

She calls you that.

ARNIE.

Well, yes.

CHRIS.

That's what I thought.

ARNIE.

She met me when I used it years ago.
I thought it best to keep the status quo.
Protect her from the industry.

CHRIS.

I see.
And now you like this new identity.

ARNIE.

I see no harm in reinventing me.

CHRIS.

But people call you by that other name.
The mail comes here for him! Do you disclaim
The checks and dividends made out to—

ARNIE.

No.
I don't care what's on my portfolio—
It can't take meetings. So, you've got to call
Me Forrest, or you won't call me at all.

CHRIS.

All right!

ARNIE.

All right! Now read this script! I need
The changes pronto. Warners has agreed
To take a meeting. We are gonna make
A killing—

CHRIS.

Which is why it's a mistake
To take on some young thing right now!

ARNIE.

Thank you
For sharing.

CHRIS.

It's what any friend would do.
Well, if you will excuse me, I'll retreat,
And get to work. What time ya wanna eat?

ARNIE.

At eight.

CHRIS.

At eight.

ARNIE.

The den is free. Use that.

CHRIS.

Okay.

ARNIE.

I'll go and see my pussycat.
I wonder if she missed me?

CHRIS.

By the way,
My brother's wife is coming in today.
Some private business. May I bring her too?

ARNIE.

Why not?

CHRIS.

I thought I'd fix her up with you.
She's lonely since my brother died last year.

ARNIE.

I'm not available.

CHRIS.

You've made that clear.

ARNIE.

Besides, she's in her forties, isn't she?

CHRIS.

A crone at least.

ARNIE.

Yeah, well, too old for me.

CHRIS.

(aside, as he leaves)

Now, to unfold a bit of strategy.

*(**CHRIS** exits, **ARNIE** goes to the neighbor's side door and rings the bell. **JORJINA** flings open a window above)*

JORJINA.

Alón! *¡La puerta!*

ALÓN.

(appearing at another window)

¿Qué?

JORJINA.

Open the door!

ALÓN.

¿Perdón?

JORJINA.

¡La puerta!

*(They both slam their windows. **ARNIE** waits.)*

ARNIE.

OK, try once more.

(The rings again. JORJINA *opens the window again.)*

JORJINA.

Alón!

ALÓN.

(flinging open his window again)

Jorjina!

BOTH.

See who's at the door!

ALÓN.

I went the last time!

JORJINA.

I went twice before!

ALÓN.

I'm busy!

JORJINA.

¡Yo también! Just go and see!

ARNIE.

Would SOMEONE open up this door for me!!??

(One more ring. Both windows fly open again.)

JORJINA.

(pretending she doesn't know who it is)

¿Quién es?

ARNIE.

Who is it! Who'd ya think!

JORJINA.

No sé.

Alón!

ALÓN.

Momento.

(to ARNIE*)*

Holá. Go away!

JORJINA.

Alón, he say go 'way.

ARNIE.

Oh, does he?

JORJINA.

Sí.

ARNIE.

Tell him to open up this door for me,
Or I will put your green cards through the shredder!
I'm waiting!

JORJINA.

Think we should?

ALÓN.

I think we better.

(They slowly come down the inside stairs, singing a little Spanish ditty. **ARNIE** *is about to explode with impatience. Finally, they enter.)*

I got it.

JORJINA.

No, I got it.

ALÓN.

No, let me!

ARNIE.

I could have shot an epic—make that three
In less time than they're taking.

JORJINA.

¡Ay, perdón!
Señor, I did not know you were—Alón!

ALÓN.

(pulling her behind him)

I make the pardon! *Señor, por favor—*
I'm sorry she did not open the door—

ARNIE.

ENOUGH!!!

(*They freeze.*)

The door is open now.

ALÓN.

That's true.

ARNIE.

So?

ALÓN.

¿Sí?

JORJINA.

¿Sí? So?

ARNIE.

Come on—tell me what's new!

JORJINA.

Not much.

ALÓN.

The weather, she is very nice.

JORJINA.

The sun shine every day—

ALÓN.

Sí, paradise.

JORJINA.

La California—

ALÓN.

Beauty like a pearl—

JORJINA.

Blue sky—

ALÓN.

Palm trees—

ARNIE.

Tell me about the girl!

JORJINA.

¿La Señorita?

ARNIE.

Sí. Yes!

ALÓN.

She's OK.

ARNIE.

You're watching her?

JORJINA.

Sí, señor, every day.

ARNIE.

Does she see anyone?

JORJINA.

Alón and me.

ARNIE.

Does she go out?

ALÓN.

Sí.

JORJINA.

On the balcony.

ARNIE.

Does she behave?

JORJINA.

Sí, like a little doll.

ALÓN.

She such a good girl.

ARNIE.

Good. Now go and call
Her out so I can talk to her.

JORJINA.

I go.

(aside to ALÓN *as she exits)*

We play with him and he don't even know!

ALÓN.

Don't worry, señor Phil, Agnès, she come.

ARNIE.

Of course she will. She's well behaved.

ALÓN.

She's dumb.

ARNIE.

Naïve.

ALÓN.

Estúpida. But sweet as flan.

ARNIE.

She loves me, doesn't she?

ALÓN.

Sí, you her man.

ARNIE.

Was she unhappy while I was away?

ALÓN.

Oh no, *señor,* she singing all the day—

(He sees **ARNIE***'s face).*

I mean, sad songs, with many tears and sighs.

ARNIE.

She misses me! That comes as no surprise.

AGNES.

(appearing on the balcony)

Yoo hoo!

ARNIE.

Yoo hoo!

AGNES.

You're back again!

ARNIE.

I'm here.

And are you glad?

AGNES.

Of course!

ARNIE.

Well, then, my dear,

My dear...

AGNES.

Yes, Uncle Phil?

ARNIE.

Have you been good?

AGNES.

Oh yes.

ARNIE.

Behaved exactly as you should?

AGNES.

Well...

ARNIE.

What!

AGNES.

It's just that in my bed at night—

ARNIE.

Your bed!—

AGNES.

They love to tickle me and bite—

ARNIE.

They do!? There's more than one!?

AGNES.

Oh yes, a lot!

ARNIE.

(aside)

My stomach's turning into one big knot—

(to her)

How did they get there?

AGNES.

Kitty brought them in.

ARNIE.

Who's Kitty!?

AGNES.

(holding up her kitten)

Mine.

ARNIE.

Let's start all over, please.

Who did this Kitty bring to you?

AGNES.

Her fleas!

ARNIE.

Her—that's what keeps you up at night?

AGNES.

Yes, sir.

ARNIE.

(aside)

Oh, God, the innocence and charm of her!
Alón!

ALÓN.

Sí!

ARNIE.

Take that kitty to the vet
And get her dipped!

ALÓN.

Yes, sir.

(He exits back into the house.)

ARNIE.

No need to fret,
My pet, we'll have you sleeping safe and snug.

AGNES.

Oh, thank you! Please come up so I can hug
The dickens out of you!

ARNIE.

Yes, I'll do that.

I'll visit soon. We'll have a little chat.

AGNES.

Oh, goody!

(She goes in.)

ARNIE.

So content with just a crumb

Of kindness. So...from top to bottom dumb.

(to audience)

Say what you will, call her obtuse or dense,

There's nothing like unbridled innocence.

*(**HAL** enters from the patio entrance, young, handsome, almost as innocent as **AGNES**. **ARNIE** sees him)*

ARNIE.

Don't tell me!

HAL.

Tell you what?

ARNIE.

I know that face!

Your father's son—I'd know you any place,

Herb!

HAL.

Hal.

ARNIE.

Right. Hal. Just out of USC.

HAL.

CalArts.

ARNIE.

Right! And you have a script for me?

HAL.

Yes, sir!

ARNIE.

That's good! In this damned industry
You gotta beat down doors with your ambition,
If you want any kind of recognition.
That's what they taught you at that fancy school,
I hope. You want all this? A swimming pool?
The house in Bu? Mercedes SUV?
The Oscar tix? Ya wanna be like me?
You gotta carpe diem, that's the way!
Just look around!

HAL.

I saw it yesterday,
Two days ago as well. I came by twice.

ARNIE.

You've seen it then! You must admit, it's nice.
Don't wait, grab every opportunity.
Network, my friend, grab meetings, hell, grab *me*!

HAL.

Yeah, thanks for all the good advice.

ARNIE.

My boy,
I have no kids myself, so it's a joy
To be a mentor to a fine young man,
To give a leg up any time I can—
Especially to children of a friend.
I'm here to help. On that you can depend.
A place to stay? A job? A—wait, I know—
I'll find you something at the studio!

HAL.

A job? That would be awesome! I could use

Some money.

ARNIE.

Well, of course. I can't refuse
My best friend's son. How 'bout a little cash
To tide you over? Help you make a splash
In Lalaland. Impress a babe or two.
Just tell old Arnie what you want to do.
Let's say a thousand bucks?

(taking out a wad and peeling off some bills)

My son, it's yours.
And use my name to get past all the doors
Of all the hot spots.

HAL.

Thanks, but—

ARNIE.

Don't be shy!
You look to me like you've got a good eye
For...indoor sports?

HAL.

I think...

ARNIE.

This town is full
Of gorgeous girls—I'm serious! No bull!
Legs up to here—so what's your pleasure, son?
I know exactly where to go for fun.
And married women! Take your choice!

HAL.

Oh, well...

ARNIE.

Go up to any door and ring the bell—
Their husbands look the other way.

HAL.

They do?

ARNIE.

It's cheaper than divorce! Of course, they too
Have fun where they can get it—catch the drift?
They've all learned more or less how they can shift
The circumstances of their dreary lives,
These lamebrains with their precious trophy wives.
So, where shall we begin? I know—my club!
Check out the merchandise in a hot tub?

HAL.

No thanks.

ARNIE.

No thanks!? Wait—don't tell me you're gay!?

HAL.

I—

ARNIE.

Listen—not to worry—it's OK,
That's fine with me—

HAL.

Well—

ARNIE.

Really! It's not bad.

HAL.

But—

ARNIE.

And don't worry. I won't tell your dad,
Until you say the word.

HAL.

I'm straight.

ARNIE.

You're straight.

HAL.

That's right.

ARNIE.

Not gay.

HAL.

Right.

ARNIE.

Then, you hesitate

Because you met someone. You've made a date!

HAL.

No, not exactly.

ARNIE.

What then?!

HAL.

Well, I've met...

A girl.

ARNIE.

All right! A looker?

HAL.

Oh, you bet.

ARNIE.

Come on, tell Uncle Arnie everything.

HAL.

She's...beautiful—

ARNIE.

Good, that's encouraging.

What else?

HAL.

She's nice—

ARNIE.

She's nice!

HAL.

And sweet—

ARNIE.

Ah, sweet!

HAL.

One look at her—

ARNIE.

She'll sweep you off your feet.

HAL.

You have to swear you'll keep this confidence!

ARNIE.

You doubt me?

HAL.

No, sir!

ARNIE.

Good.

(*aside*)

I'm in suspense—

Whose wife has strayed into the arms of this
Good-looking stud? Whose pleasant hours of bliss
Will soon be shattered by the rumors spread
All over town? Who got him into bed!?

(*to him*)

My son, I know too well the value of
Discretion in the face of secret love.
Who is she?

HAL.

Just an angel, nothing less.

ARNIE.

I'm sure.

HAL.

With such a smile, I must confess
I'm forced to tremble when she flashes it.

ARNIE.

A smile is so important.

HAL.

I admit
She'll seem a bit naïve right at the start—

ARNIE.

I see.

HAL.

But when you see inside her...heart,
You'll be won over.

ARNIE.

Will I?

HAL.

There's a dimple
On her chin.

ARNIE.

Is there?

HAL.

You'd call her simple—

ARNIE.

Would I?

HAL.

But this precious naiveté
Is just what made me love her right away.

ARNIE.

It would.

HAL.

I loved her from the very first.

ARNIE.

You loved—

(aside)

My head is just about to burst—

(to him, hoarsely)

Where does she live?

HAL.

You won't believe it.

ARNIE.

Try me.

HAL.

Next door to you!

ARNIE.

Imagine that—right by me!

HAL.

Her name is—

(**ARNIE** *mouths it with him, looking away*)

Agnes.

ARNIE.

Agnes.

HAL.

It's old fashioned,
But I don't care. My heart is so impassioned,
I sing it day and night—

BOTH.

(singing, in harmony)

Agnès, Agnès!

HAL.

My life is filled with joy—

ARNIE.

(aside)

My life's a mess.
Oh God, I leave for two weeks and some hunk
Moves in on her! If Chris finds out, I'm sunk.
It only takes one word to start the talk.
If it gets out, I'll be the laughing stock
Of everyone from Eastwood down to Moore.
In one week I'll be Arnie, the obscure,
Goodbye, Phil Forrest, paragon of men,
I'll never eat lunch in this town again!

HAL.

Are you all right? You look a little gray.

ARNIE.

Just tired. It's been such a stressful day.
But tell me, why the secrecy with her?

HAL.

(looking around, then whispering)

Because, my darling is a prisoner!

ARNIE.

No!

HAL.

There's this creep who's locked her in that house!
She's not allowed outside, poor little mouse,
While Woods, no Forrest, that's the fellow's name,
Tells my sweet darling that he's got some claim
To her.

ARNIE.

Disgusting.

HAL.

Do you know this jerk?

ARNIE.

Oh, yes.

HAL.

Oh good! Then maybe you can work
On our behalf, convince the nitwit to
Give up his claim.

ARNIE.

I'll see what I can do.

HAL.

Oh, thank you, sir! My father said you'd be
A good friend. This means everything to me.

ARNIE.

And me. But tell me, has this ingénue

Done anything to prove her love for you?

HAL.

Oh yes!

ARNIE.

She has? Please, tell me what she's done.

HAL.

Let's see...she smiled at me...

ARNIE.

(*aside*)

Where is my gun...?

HAL.

She waved, I waved, she waved—

ARNIE.

(*aside*)

This kid is odd.

(*to him*)

Have you gone in...her room?

HAL.

Not yet.

ARNIE.

Thank God!

I mean—that's good—no rush—

HAL.

I know I'll get

Up there, somehow—

ARNIE.

Arrgghh!

HAL.

– Get myself inside

That house and win her love!

ARNIE.

(*aside*)

I'm crucified.

HAL.

And look at this! A thousand! That will do
For starters!

ARNIE.

Ah, the money I gave you.

HAL.

I'll bribe those guards with this— I'm sure to win!

ARNIE.

(aside)

I gave him ready cash to do me in.

HAL.

Boy, you look pretty bad.

ARNIE.

I do feel ill.

HAL.

I'll go. You'll keep our secret?

ARNIE.

That I will.

HAL.

Especially not my father—he can't know!

ARNIE.

Not him or anyone.

HAL.

I've got to go!
Thanks, once again.

(He exits.)

ARNIE.

Excruciating pain
Surrounds the central cortex of my brain.
The irony! He blabbed the whole affair
To the one man with whom he shouldn't share
A single detail! And I had to sit

And listen to him call me a nitwit,
And bare his plan to steal my future bride.
AND, I will have to put my pride aside
And play the game to keep his confidence,
So I can come up with my own defense.
Which I will do! I've been through worse than this—
I weathered *Waterworld and The Abyss,*
The shakeup at the studio—I won!
But how to finish what this kid's begun!?

    (He strides over to the fence)

Alón! Jorjina!

    (Two windows fly open)

ALÓN & JORJINA.

  ¿Sí?

ARNIE.

You let him come
To steal my fiancée!! My face is numb.

ALÓN.

A man!?

JORJINA.

Come in here!?

ARNIE.

Not another word!
I'm sweating like a pig. My speech is slurred.
If I weren't in the middle of a stroke
I'd put my hands round both your necks and choke!
Get down here!

    (They start to gibber in Spanish.)

  NOW!

    (They slam the windows and come down the stairs, chattering in Spanish. They enter.)

      He saw her! He got past

The two of you! He must run very fast!
Of course he does. He's young…and ripped, and strong.
Well? Did he simply ring the bell—ding-dong,
And you said, "*Buenos días, ¿cómo está?*
Come in and meet la chica bonita?"
Where did they meet? Were they alone? Oh hell,
Why didn't you just call me on the cell!?
I'll go ask her. She'll tell me everything
That happened to her. Oh, I'm suffering!

ALÓN.

Qué lástima, señor.

JORJINA.

Something not good.

ARNIE.

(*barely under control*)

I think perhaps you both misunderstood
Your duties.

JORJINA.

No, *señor*!

ALÓN.

We understand!

JORJINA.

We do all of those things that you demand!
We watch *la señorita*—

ALÓN.

Like the hawk—

ARNIE.

And yet, *la señorita* had a talk—

JORJINA.

Oh *sí*, she step out on her balcony—

ALÓN.

She talk to everybody that she see!

The niños and the viejos—

JORJINA.

She so sweet,

She say hello to people in the street.

The dogs and cats—

ARNIE.

I—

ALÓN.

All the birds and bees—

ARNIE.

But—

JORJINA.

Even to the flowers and the trees!

"*Holá*, you trees!"

ALÓN.

"*Holá*, you birds!"

ARNIE.

ALL RIGHT!

But no young men. Just keep her out of sight

Of all young men who hang around.

JORJINA & ALÓN.

Okay.

ARNIE.

I'd better hear what she has got to say.

Could be he never spoke to her! Why not?

I'll figure out if she's part of the plot.

But first I've got to go spruce up a bit

And calm down! She can't see me in a fit.

(He exits into the house.)

ALÓN.

(returning to his normal voice)

I can't keep doing this.

JORJINA.

Of course you can.

We both agreed, it's all part of the plan
To keep him from this big mistake.

ALÓN.

I know.

But I don't see where this is gonna go.

JORJINA.

El Señor Chris will fix it. He is wise.
So you just keep the ball upon your eyes
And do exactly what he says.

ALÓN.

OK!

Aiee, Dios mio, what a crazy day.
Es loco de atar, this Hollywood.

JORJINA.

We'll write a script when it's all over.

ALÓN.

Good!

(**CHRIS** *appears on the opposite balcony, talking on his cell*)

CHRIS.

You two!

ALÓN & JORJINA.

Sí!

CHRIS.

What's her name?

ALÓN & JORJINA.

Agnès.

CHRIS.

I know.

I mean her LAST name!

ALÓN & JORJINA.

Oh.

CHRIS.

Go find out.

(They hesitate.)

GO!

I'll stall him out here. Hurry up!

ALÓN & JORJINA.

OK!

CHRIS.

OK, now to advance this passion play.

*(**ALÓN** and **JORJINA** hurry into the guest house as **ARNIE** re-enters, spruced up, splashing cologne on his face.)*

CHRIS.

Hey Arnie!

ARNIE.

Phil!

CHRIS.

All right, Phil. How's that deal

With Spielberg going? Is he gonna steal

Antonio from you for his new pic?

ARNIE.

Don't know yet.

CHRIS.

Well, you'd better make it quick—

ARNIE.

(aside)

I wish you'd make it quick—

(To him)

Chris, why don't you

Just go and read?

CHRIS.

Right. That's what I should do.

You're trying to get rid of me!

ARNIE.

Baloney.

I've got a conference call with Fox and Sony.

I need some privacy.

CHRIS.

Okay, I'll read

But call me if there's anything you need.

ARNIE.

Right.

(He grabs a script and exits into the house. **ALÓN** *and* **JORJINA** *enter.)*

CHRIS.

Well?

JORJINA.

She don't know her last name!

CHRIS.

I'll try

And get it. Meanwhile, find a good P.I.,

To snoop around, ask questions, point the way.

ALÓN.

We know somebody, up near Monterey.

JORJINA.

Alón! You don't mean—

ALÓN.

Why not?

ALÓN & JORJINA.

Uncle Juan!

JORJINA.

But—

ALÓN.

Uncle Juan knows how to get things done.

JORJINA.

I know!

CHRIS.

Good! Get him started. Right away!
With luck we'll get the crisis solved today.

JORJINA.

OK!

ALÓN.

OK!

(They go back into the guest house.)

CHRIS.

OK. Whoops—here he is!

*(**ARNIE** re-enters, making a beeline for **AGNES**' door)*

CHRIS.

Well? How are tricks at Fox?

ARNIE.

Oh, same old biz.

CHRIS.

No doubt. *(pause)* Soooo, Agnes. What's her other name?

ARNIE.

Her other name?

CHRIS.

Her last name.

ARNIE.

What's this game?
Why do you want to know?

CHRIS.

Just curious.

ARNIE.

I...don't remember.

CHRIS.

Right.

ARNIE.

What's all the fuss?

Why do you care? She's Agnes, just like Cher.

And now, excuse me, she is waiting there,

And you're impeding progress. GO AND READ!

CHRIS.

Of course, Phil.

(aside, as he leaves)

Now it's time to intercede.

ARNIE.

OK, at last!

(calling up)

Oh, Agnes, Agnes dear?

AGNES.

(appearing at the window)

Yes?

ARNIE.

(aside)

Look at her!

(to her)

Would you please come down here?

AGNES.

All right! I'm coming!

*(She closes the window and we hear her childlike steps descending as she sings, badly. **ARNIE** primps a little, sucks in his gut and poses. She appears.)*

Here I am!

ARNIE.

Hello!

(He opens his arms, she runs into them, like she's greeting her favorite uncle, and plants a kiss on his cheek. He holds on to her for dear life.)

AGNES.

I can't breathe!

ARNIE.

(releasing her)

Sorry.

(He paces a little, then looks at her.)

Well, you're all…aglow.
Has something happened?

AGNES.

Happened? I don't know.

ARNIE.

What kept you occupied while I was gone?

AGNES.

Oh, lots of things! The sewing—

ARNIE.

And? Go on.

AGNES.

The…cooking!

ARNIE.

Cooking! What else did you do?

AGNES.

I…don't remember!

ARNIE.

Is it true that you
Conversed with someone?

AGNES.

Yes!

ARNIE.

Who!?

AGNES.

Lots of folks!
A little girl, an old man who told jokes—

I'll tell you one...um...

ARNIE.

Then I was right!
A neighbor told me he had seen a sight
So unbelievable, I said no way.
You talking to a young man yesterday!
I bet him 50 bucks he was mistaken.

AGNES.

You did?

ARNIE.

I did.

AGNES.

That's too bad. You got taken.

ARNIE.

You mean it's true?

AGNES.

As true as it can be!

ARNIE.

You talked to him?

AGNES.

And he talked back to me!

ARNIE.

Now isn't that exciting! Tell me, dear,
How it all happened. I can't wait to hear!

AGNES.

And when you hear it, you'll know I did right.
Why, thinking of it gives me such a fright!

ARNIE.

Poor darling!

AGNES.

I was on the balcony,
Just sitting in the sunshine, there was me,
Enjoying all of nature's wonders rare,

The trees, the bees, the birds, the morning air—

ARNIE.

It was a lovely day—

AGNES.

I looked around,
And then, by chance, my eyes dropped to the ground,
And there was this young man! He waved and smiled,
And so I waved and smiled.

ARNIE.

Delightful child.

Continue.

AGNES.

Well, I couldn't walk away,
That would be rude!

ARNIE.

Of course! You had to stay.

AGNES.

That's right! He waved again, and smiled to boot.
Well, what else could I do? I followed suit
And smiled right back at him. And waved again.
He smiled and waved, I waved and smiled...and then...
I think he smiled once more and went away.

ARNIE.

And that was all?

AGNES.

Uh-huh. Until next day,
I go out on the balcony to greet
The morning—oh, the air was very sweet,
That next day, with the birds, the bees, the air,
I look down, and my goodness, standing there,
Where he had stood the day before, I see
An old, old woman. She looks up at me,
Says, "Bless you, señorita." "Bless you too,"
I say. Then she says, "I must talk to you,"

She says to me, "El Dios gave you beauty,
So I must do for Him my sacred duty
And tell you that you've wounded someone." "Oh!"
I say. But how this happened I don't know.
Perhaps I dropped a pot on someone's head
And split it open. Someone might be dead!
"What did I do!?" "*Sus ojos...*" "What?" "Your eyes,"
She said, "Are weapons to effect the sad demise
Of any man who sees them." "Is that true?"
I asked. She nods. "Oh, dear, what should I do!?"
"You must agree to see the man whose heart
From one look in your eyes is torn apart,
For nothing but a kindly look from you
Can save him from the torment he's been through."
"That's all I have to do?" "That's all," says she.
"Well, shoot, that's nothin', send him right to me."
Why, I'd be crueler than the cruelest cad
If I did not agree. "*Sí*, I am glad,"
She says. "He'll come to you tomorrow.
One look from you will banish all his sorrow,"
And so it was! He came and looked and ping!
He cheered right up! It made me want to sing.

(She sings, badly, then looks at **ARNIE**)

You look a little peekid. Was I wrong
To help him? Oh, you didn't like the song!
Well, you know how I am. I just can't bear
To think of someone suffering. There,
You've got to smile for me, or else I'll cry,
If I thought I had hurt you, I would die!

(He manages a forced smile)

ARNIE.

(aside)

Oh God, why did I ever go away?

(*to her*)

Is that it, dear? That's all you have to say?

AGNES.

Uh-huh.

ARNIE.

So it was just a conversation.

AGNES.

Well...

ARNIE.

Aarghh!

(*aside*)

Stay calm. So far, no assignation.

AGNES.

He gave me—

ARNIE.

What!?

AGNES.

A book of poetry.

ARNIE.

A book of—

AGNES.

Poems, he wrote just for me!

You want to hear one?

ARNIE.

Yes, that would be great.

AGNES.

Let's see, here's one. "Your lips are like"—Oh wait!
There's one that's better—it's an elegy!
It's called—you'll love this—"On Her Balcony."

(*She recites:*)

"She stands up there, so far above,

So near and yet so far, my love,

Two arms reach out, not far enough,

The distance is so very tough.

I climb into her sweet embrace,

My lips are on her neck and face"—

ARNIE.

(aside)

Her neck and face!?

AGNES.

"I pay the price

Of entry into Paradise."

He's very good!

ARNIE.

I see his name in lights.

AGNES.

So full of...truth.

ARNIE.

I'll buy the movie rights.

Of course that scene's in his imagination.

AGNES.

Oh no!

ARNIE.

It has to be a fabrication.

AGNES.

That's just the way it happened. In our dreams.

ARNIE.

Oh.

(aside)

Good, there's still some time. I need new schemes

To keep the two of them apart.

(to her)

My dear,

You've been a good girl. I am glad to hear
He didn't take—

AGNES.

Oh, yes he did!

ARNIE.

Took what!?

AGNES.

You'll be so angry.

ARNIE.

No! Just tell me.

AGNES.

But,

I know you. You get awfully mad sometimes.

ARNIE.

I promise. Not if it's the worst of crimes!

AGNES.

He took my—

ARNIE.

(aside)

Oh God, here it comes!

AGNES.

Barrette.

The pink one that you gave me. You're upset.

ARNIE.

The pink barrette! I'm not upset. I'm fine.
But you must promise to avoid this swine.
The fellow is a dirty rotten bum.

AGNES.

Oh, no he's not!

ARNIE.

He is, the man is scum,

Not to be trusted.

AGNES.

But he swore to me
His love would last through all eternity!
The things he said and did, they made me feel
All tingly on the inside. I just squeal—

(she does)

Each time I think of it. Until that day
I didn't know that I could feel that way!

ARNIE.

You can't.

AGNES.

I can't?

ARNIE.

Unless you are a wife.
You must be married, otherwise your life
Is pure and unadulterated sin.
At Heaven's Gate, they'd never let you in.

AGNES.

Oh, no. I'm very sad.

ARNIE.

Not for too long.

AGNES.

But I don't understand why it's so wrong
To feel that way, so sweet, so very pleasant!
I felt like God had given me a present!
Why can't I— WAIT! If I was married, then
I'd be allowed to feel that way again!!??

ARNIE.

As often as I—you wish.

AGNES.

Well, then, all right,
Can I get married?

ARNIE.

Yes, you can—tonight.

AGNES.

Tonight! Oh, Uncle Phil! It can't be true!

ARNIE.

It's why I came back early. Just for you.

AGNES.

You angel!

(She flies into his arms and hugs him.)

ARNIE.

There'll be many more of those!

AGNES.

I need a dress! I can't wear these old clothes.

ARNIE.

I'll send for something.

AGNES.

Oh, my hair's a mess!

ARNIE.

My only wish is for your happiness.
I'll bring a stylist from the studio.
But, we must keep it simple—no big show.

AGNES.

Oh, dearest Uncle Phil, straight from my heart,
How can I thank you?

ARNIE.

Drop the uncle part.

AGNES.

I'll be beholden to you all my life,
Imagine, years of joy as that man's wife!

ARNIE.

That man?

AGNES.

Hal!

ARNIE.

Hal! Now, let me get this straight.

You think I picked out Hal to be your mate?

AGNES.

Why, sure! That's just exactly what you said—

ARNIE.

I did? No, there's a better man instead.
As for that other worthless jerk you met,
From here on in, you're going to forget
You ever saw him.

AGNES.

Oh, I can't do that!

ARNIE.

You can, you must, you will, my pussycat.
You've got to promise me, if he comes here,
Under no circumstance will you appear

(handing her a little rock)

To him, except to throw this rock and say,
"I never want to see you—go away!"

AGNES.

But I—

ARNIE.

No more protesting—that's enough!
No sympathy for him. You must hang tough!

(She bursts into tears.)

Oh, don't do that, I'm just reminding you,
That you're a good girl, and what you must do
Is listen and obey, just like they taught
You at your school. That's what you ought
To do, now, isn't it? So, dry your eyes,
You're young, and in this matter, I am wise.
In all things I am wise. You have to trust
That I will make decisions that are just.
Stop crying, now.

AGNES.

(bursting into tears again)

All right!

ARNIE.

Look at me, dear.
Head up, come on, I only want to cheer
You up a bit. I know you feel…confused—

AGNES.

(pointing to her chest)

It hurts right there—

ARNIE.

I know, your heart is bruised,
But you must trust that all will be all right,
That you'll be happy once again tonight
When you meet your fiancé. Dear, you see,
You thought he'd be a stranger, but it's…me.

AGNES.

You!?

ARNIE.

Yes. Your own sweet Phil.

AGNES.

YOU!???

ARNIE.

Yes! It's true.

AGNES.

You want to MARRY me!?

ARNIE.

I do, I do.
So happy you can't speak— I understand.
The judge will come tonight, you'll take my hand
And we'll be joined in wedlock. Do you see?
As of tonight you will belong to me.

So, go upstairs, wait for the creep. And when
He comes, shout to him, "Don't come here again!"
And throw the stone right at his head.

AGNES.

Oh no!

Not at his head!

ARNIE.

Between the eyes, pronto!

AGNES.

His eyes are beautiful…

ARNIE.

Forget his eyes.
From now on, baby, I'm your lucky prize.
You'll soon forget that other slob, like that!

AGNES.

I never will!

ARNIE.

Now, listen, pussycat—

AGNES.

I'm not a pussycat!

ARNIE.

My twinkling star!

Remember?

(singing)

HOW I WONDER WHERE YOU ARE?
WE USED TO PLAY THAT GAME WHEN I WOULD VISIT!
YOU'D HIDE, I'D FIND YOU AND WE'D LAUGH—EXQUISITE!
I WAS YOUR FEARLESS KNIGHT—YOU WERE MY QUEEN!

AGNES.

Yes. I was eight then. Now I'm seventeen.

*(She goes in the house and shuts the door. In a musical
interlude, with flickering old time movie lights **ARNIE**
hides, **AGNES** comes out on the balcony as **HAL** appears
below. She starts to wave, sees **ARNIE** and changes her*

expression to a scowl, throws the stone and hits him in the head. He yelps with pain and she busts into tears again. **HAL** *picks up the stone and exits,* **AGNES** *exits thru the balcony)*

ARNIE.

Well, that went well. I'm sure she'll come around.

All right, I may have lost a little ground,

But she will learn to love me, I am sure.

A very hasty marriage is the cure.

(going to the guest house)

Alón! Jorjina!

ALÓN & JORJINA.

(as the door flies open immediately and they enter)

¿Sí?

ARNIE.

We're all in danger.

ALÓN.

We are?

ARNIE.

Yes! You remember that young stranger

Who tried to get inside the house?

JORJINA.

Sí.

ALÓN.

Sí.

ARNIE.

Now, listen very carefully to me.

The man's a thief.

ALÓN & JORJINA.

No!

ARNIE.

Yes.

JORJINA.

How do you know?

ARNIE.

He robbed a bank in Boise, Idaho.

ALÓN.

Caramba!

ARNIE.

There, too.

ALÓN.

Call the FBI!

ARNIE.

No, no! We don't need them, just keep an eye—
A careful one—on my young lady. See
He doesn't try to get past you or me.
He's just the type to take advantage of
A sweet young thing who's never been in love.
I've made enough B movies, I should know
A villain when I see one. We must go
To any lengths to stop him. Diligence
Is what we need to guard her innocence!
Don't let her stray one inch out of your sight,
Until we're married, which will be tonight.
Now, go and get her. Bring her down to me.

*(They run off. During the next monologue, he primps
himself again, pours a stiff drink and a soda for* **AGNES***)*

This one will need some tact and subtlety.
She's still close to perfection, moldable,
I've simply got to keep her worshipful
And uninformed about the world. Then she
Will have to learn...well...everything from me.
What worldly woman would succumb to that?
One small dissent, she turns into a cat
With claws unsheathed, prepared for the attack,
Like Batman's babe, she gives the whip a crack

And we give in. Or else she needles you,
Manipulates so cunningly that you
Do just the thing you didn't want to do.
Then there's the ones who argue. Till you're hoarse
You bicker, shout and try to stay your course
With reason, logic, all to no avail.
You capsize anyway, a huge, beached whale.

(He checks his image in the glass window.)

We men have got to stay at the controls!
Or else we risk the murder of our souls!
It's why so many marriages turn sour.
The wife is young and sweet, but by the hour
She learns about the way things are out there.
Before you know it, she begins to care
About things other than the man she wed,
Like shopping, and it goes right to her head!
At that point, you are doomed. You might as well
Just buy a one way ticket straight to hell!
Well, not yours truly—I have planned too long
To have some schmuck make it turn out all wrong!

(He takes out his cell and dials.)

Phil Forrest. Put me through to my attorney.
I said right now—don't give me any—Bernie!

(He waits a moment.)

I need you right away. I'll send my man
To get you. Fifteen minutes— yes, you can!
You're going to marry us tonight! That's right.
Don't argue pal, I'm ready for a fight—
Who got you on the bench, your honor? Well,
Don't argue—I don't want to have to yell—
You owe me one. Don't grunt, say yes and smile!
I promise you I'll make it worth your while.

(ALÓN and JORJINA re-enter with AGNES. She is holding the book of poetry)

Alón, pick up the judge at this address—

(hands him a slip of paper)

Jorjina, clean the living room, then press
The white Versace suit.

(They both exit, chattering in Spanish again.)

And now, my dear,
Let go of that.

(He pries with great difficulty the poetry book from her hand, then hands her the soda.)

Good. Come right over here.
Sit. Very good. Look up at me. That's right.
Please listen, dear, though your attention might
Begin to wander to some other place.

AGNES.

What other place?

ARNIE.

Just look into my face.
Well, sweetheart, we should talk about...uh...fate.
You know what fate is?

AGNES.

No.

ARNIE.

(as he mixes himself a drink and gives her a soda from the bar)

I'll demonstrate.
We meet. You are a child, I am a man.
Yet, somehow, I know God has wrought a plan
To bring us two together in a way
That's special and unique. What can I say?
You were a poor and ignorant young thing,

And with my wealth and power I could bring
A host of new experiences to
An underprivileged creature such as you.
I thought that when you'd finally grown to be
The luscious—lovely—creature that I see
Before me, then your gratitude would make
You want to heed my wishes for my sake.

AGNES.

(who has never tasted soda)

What's this?

ARNIE.

A soda.

AGNES.

Oh. I like it.

ARNIE.

Good.

Now, Agnes, there's a few things that we should
Discuss.

AGNES.

Hal?

ARNIE.

No.

AGNES.

Oh. What then?

ARNIE.

Something nice.

AGNES.

Hal!

ARNIE.

No!

AGNES.

Well, what then!?

ARNIE.

Paradise!

AGNES.

You mean like Heaven?

ARNIE.

Yes.

AGNES.

Okay.

ARNIE.

Good. Fine.

So. Heaven will be ours when you are mine.
My wife. You know what that word might entail?

AGNES.

Uh-uh.

ARNIE.

Well, then, I will explain. The male,
That's me, takes you, a female, for his mate.
He cares for her, which then will obligate
The female, you, to bow to his desires,
Whatever they may be. If he requires
A service, she performs it. She's his wife.
And so I must advise you of the life
You'll live once you're my spouse. A life that's good,
Providing you do everything you should
To please your husband. Marriage is no joke,
It's serious—put down the Diet Coke—
For years I shunned it. Women on the make
Tried hard to snare me. But make no mistake,
I had a vision of my wife-to-be,
And there you are, the soul of purity,
All pink and ripe and ready to obey
Your husband's wishes.

AGNES.

Wishes? What are they?

ARNIE.

Just to agree with everything I say.

There's one more thing, and that's the wedding night.

It's really nothing, there's no cause for fright

Or panic. Anything you may have heard

Is pure exaggeration. How absurd!

No need to fear it. It's a little thing,

It really is, not worth considering.

But this you must consider. Till tonight

Your conduct must be absolutely right,

Which means not speaking to a single man.

Can you do that for me? I'm sure you can.

No one at all. That is what you must do.

If someone tries to talk to you? Adieu!

Just point your finger, show him where to go.

Right out the door this minute! Just say no.

AGNES.

No!

ARNIE.

Good, you're practicing.

AGNES.

No!

ARNIE.

That was better.

(aside)

She follows everything right to the letter!

CHRIS.

(calling from offstage)

Hey, Phil!

ARNIE.

Now what!

(to **AGNES** *)*

Go back inside!

AGNES.

All right.

(She grabs the poetry book and runs back into her little prison)

ARNIE.

(aside)

Oh God, just keep me going till tonight!

CHRIS.

(entering)

The blushing bride.

ARNIE.

Yes.

CHRIS.

Very appetizing.

And have you sampled yet?

ARNIE.

No.

CHRIS.

That's surprising.

ARNIE.

Well, as it happens, I'll take my first bite
By ten PM tonight.

CHRIS.

Tonight!?

ARNIE.

That's right.

And you're my witness.

CHRIS.

You want me to watch!?

ARNIE.

The *wedding.*

CHRIS.

Oh. I think I need a scotch.

Want one?

ARNIE.

God, yes.

CHRIS.

Shall I call in some guests

To share the joy?

ARNIE.

No! Wedding guests are pests.

CHRIS.

And is the bride prepared for nuptial bliss?

ARNIE.

Of course.

CHRIS.

She didn't look so keen to kiss

When I was in the living room.

ARNIE.

Her hair.

You know how girls are.

HAL.

(from offstage)

Arnie! Are you there?

ARNIE.

(aside)

Oh God, I can't let these two meet!

(to **CHRIS***)*

Chris!!

CHRIS.

What??

ARNIE.

(taking keys from his pocket)

Here, take the Jag. Go to the ***Coif and Cut,***

It's on Rodeo Drive. Bring back Pierre!

CHRIS.

Who's Pierre?

ARNIE.

The guy who's gonna do her hair!
Then Guess.

CHRIS.

What?

ARNIE.

Guess!

CHRIS.

Oh, I don't want to guess.

ARNIE.

The clothing store!

CHRIS.

Ah.

ARNIE.

Go and buy a dress!

CHRIS.

A dress at Guess?

ARNIE.

A wardrobe. Everything!
Then Cartier. Get an engagement ring—

HAL.

(Still offstage)

Where are you?

CHRIS.

Who's that?

ARNIE.

Just some stupid bore.

(to HAL)

I'm on the phone—wait there—

(to CHRIS)

She's a size four—

The dress. The ring—make it five carats–

CHRIS.

Wow.

HAL.

(perilously close to entering)

Oh, you're still on the patio—

ARNIE.

(to **CHRIS***)*

GO NOW!!!

*(***CHRIS*** goes as* **HAL** *enters from opposite stage, with a bandage on his head.* **ARNIE** *turns and faces him calmly.* **CHRIS** *sneaks back and eavesdrops.)*

Hello again.

HAL.

Hey, here you are!

ARNIE.

What's new?

How goes the big romance? Did you get through

The barricade and see your sweetheart?

HAL.

Yes.

But not without an awful lot of stress.

ARNIE.

What happened?

HAL.

Seven stitches for a start.

(He shows him his scalp.)

ARNIE.

Oh, that looks bad.

HAL.

Not so bad as my heart.

ARNIE.

Oh, that sounds bad.

HAL.

It is. You'll never guess.
The old guy's back and trying to oppress
My sweetheart.

ARNIE.

Oh, that IS bad.

HAL.

And, he's on

To us.

ARNIE.

He is?

HAL.

That ancient mastodon—

ARNIE.

He must be very old—

HAL.

Compared to her?

A relic.

ARNIE.

How do you plan to deter
His actions?

HAL.

I don't know. First, I'll get past
Those two he hired as guards. They're holding fast,
Like it's a fort or something.

ARNIE.

They said no?

HAL.

In no uncertain terms. I turned to go,
When she appeared up on the balcony,

She raised her arm, I thought, to wave at me,
And BAM! This boulder hit me in the head.

ARNIE.

How terrible.

HAL.

I'm lucky I'm not dead.

ARNIE.

You're right.

HAL.

A doctor sewed me up, and then,
I thought I would go back and try again—

ARNIE.

Again!?

HAL.

I staggered down the street to rest—

ARNIE.

At that point, yes, a rest would be the best.

HAL.

I thought I'd clear my mind and take a walk,
And then I noticed, I still had the rock!

ARNIE.

The rock!

HAL.

The one that had just left her hand,
And then I saw this—

(He holds up an object.)

ARNIE.

This? A rubber band?
Where did that come from?

HAL.

Right around the stone.

ARNIE.

That's odd, I don't remember—

HAL.

It was thrown

By my sweet, clever girl with this around it!

(He holds up a piece of paper.)

A note from her!

ARNIE.

How lucky that you found it!

(aside)

Oh God, I've got a pain in my left arm!

Breathe deep. There's no cause yet for great alarm—

She went against my orders!

(to him)

What's it say?

(He grabs the letter, **HAL** *grabs it back.)*

HAL.

No! No one touches this but me.

ARNIE.

Okay!

You read.

HAL.

This letter is what proved to me

She didn't mean to cause me injury,

But he had forced her! Watched her, probably.

ARNIE.

You think so?

HAL.

There is nothing he won't try

To steal her from me. But I'd rather die

Than quit.

ARNIE.

By all means, fight him to the death!

(aside)

And please let me be there for his last breath!

(to him)

But read!

HAL.

It starts...you know, love is a jewel
That makes saints out of sinners. The most cruel
Bad-ass old creep can turn into a kind,
Compass'nate human being.

ARNIE.

Love is blind.

HAL.

I think if this old fart could really see
How much in love we are, he'd set her free.

ARNIE.

The letter.

HAL.

Right. Let's see, where did I start?

ARNIE.

You didn't.

HAL.

Oh. See that? She put a heart
Right at the top!

ARNIE.

How sweet. What does she SAY!?

HAL.

She says, "My dearest—" don't you think she's clever
About the note? Would you imagine—

ARNIE.

Never.

HAL.

— That she, so innocent, would think of that?

ARNIE.

It blows my mind.

HAL.

My little pussycat.

ARNIE.

Your what!?

HAL.

A nickname.

ARNIE.

And she likes it?

HAL.

Yes.

She'll purr like one the first time I caress
Her—

ARNIE.

Read the goddam letter!

HAL.

Here I go!

"My dearest, sweetest—"

ARNIE.

I don't want to know.

HAL.

You don't?

ARNIE.

No. Yes!

HAL.

You really care about
My girl and me and how it all turns out,
Don't you?

ARNIE.

More than you'll ever know, my boy.
So, read the letter. Let us both enjoy
The passion in her poetry.

HAL.

(He reads the following with great difficulty, as most of it is NOT in iambic pentameter.)

"My dearest, sweetest Hal, what can I say?
I threw a rock and made you go away,
But what I really wanted was for you to stay.
Except I couldn't tell you that out loud.
My guardian tells me I am not ever allowed
To talk to you again. I don't know why,
But thinking of it makes me want to really really cry.
I'm all filled up with feelings and I don't
Know what they mean, except that I won't
Get into Heaven if I feel them and
I'm still not married. I don't really understand
Why not, but I sure want to get married soon,
But not to some old raccoon.
I really would prefer to be married to
Someone who makes me feel like this—like you
Do. So even though my guardian tells me that
You're just a big fat liar, I say, he's not fat!
And he is not a liar. He is nice.
And smart. That's why I'm asking for your advice.
Should I just go and marry that old guy,
Or is there someone else who might be willing to try?"

(They both wipe their eyes. **CHRIS** *appears on the patio, unseen by* **ARNIE***, and hides behind a palm.)*

Is that the sweetest thing you ever heard?

ARNIE.

Sheer poetry.

HAL.

I tell you, every word
Is etched upon my heart.

ARNIE.

Mine too.

But, son, what is it that you plan to do?

HAL.

I don't know yet, but something big—you're choking!

ARNIE.

I know. I've got to try and give up smoking.

HAL.

I'll get you something cold to drink.

ARNIE.

No, no!

I've got a meeting, so you need to go.

Right now.

HAL.

Okay. And I should go and plot

My next attack.

(He exits.)

ARNIE.

Arrgghh! Pompous little snot!

HAL.

(returning)

But since you live next door, could you suggest

A way to—

ARNIE.

Not now! I am very stressed!

HAL.

Man, Hollywood can really bring you down.

I think you should get out of Tinseltown

A while.

ARNIE.

Goodbye!

(HAL exits as ALÓN and JORJINA sneak in US, unseen by ARNIE. They stand and watch and listen.)

ARNIE.

He is the most clue-free

Jackass I've ever seen! Yet he could be

The one to screw me without even trying!

How he usurped my power is stupefying!

(Lights down on **ARNIE**; **CHRIS**, **ALÓN** *and* **JORJINA** *convene.)*

CHRIS.

He wouldn't tell me. Now it's up to you.

JORJINA.

If he won't tell you, what we gonna do?

CHRIS.

I have a plan.

ALÓN.

A plot!

JORJINA.

A strategy!

CHRIS.

To get her out of—

ALÓN, JORJINA & CHRIS.

That man's custody!

(Lights down on them, up on **ARNIE**)*

ARNIE.

And she! The way she looked at me and smiled,

As guilt-free as that innocent young child

She once was. And that paragon of flirts

Looks so intensely beautiful it hurts.

She…glows. She twinkles— radiates a light!

But not because I am her shining knight.

(lights down on **ARNIE**, *up on* **CHRIS**, **ALÓN** *and* **JORJINA**)*

CHRIS.

Good, that takes care of my part. Now to you—

The two of you—here's what you have to do:

(He whispers to them.)

ALÓN.

No.

(more whispering)

NO! I can't!

JORJINA.

(seducing him)

Oh yes you can.

ALÓN.

I can?

JORJINA.

(still seducing him)

You betcha.

CHRIS.

Absolutely.

JORJINA.

You the man.

CHRIS.

Meanwhile I'd better go and get Pierre.

JORJINA.

Who's Pierre?

CHRIS.

The guy who's gonna do her hair.

(Lights down on them, up on ARNIE.)

ARNIE.

Why can't she glow like that just once for me!?
For thirteen years she's been in custody.
I could have left her starving on that farm,
But no, not me. "Come, sweetheart, take my arm
And I'll take care of you forever more!"
She has her fill, then boots me out the door
For some young shithead! I can't take these panics.
I've got to get my bearings—where's my Xanax!?

(Lights down on **ARNIE**. **AGNES** *comes out on her balcony, crying.* **HAL** *enters below it and looks up at her; lights on them)*

HAL.

Oh, Agnes!

AGNES.

Hal! You are so far away!

HAL.

So far away!? Wait! Wait! How can I say...

(He pulls out a tablet and begins scribbling, speaking as he writes.)

(reading her his latest poem)

"The day is cold, and oh, so gray,
Since you, my darling, went away.
I want you back without delay,
My dearest, sweetest fiancée,
So we can make a getaway.
Please marry me, my love."

AGNES.

Okay!

(lights up on **ARNIE***)*

ARNIE.

Goddammit, I spent fortunes on that honey
Of a girl. But no, it's not the money...
It's pride. And what the tabloids all will say
About me and my teenage fiancée.

CHRIS.

(stepping out on the patio, shaking his head in frustration)

Oh, Phil!

AGNES.

Oh Hal!

HAL.

Oh, Agnes!

JORJINA.

*(as **ALÓN** grabs her)*

Oh, Alón!

ALÓN.

Jorjina…

ARNIE.

Oh my head. What's going on!?
Why has my life turned into a B movie?

CHRIS.

Don't worry—help is on the way.

ALÓN & JORJINA.

(making out)

That's groovy!

ARNIE.

I'll be the butt of everyone's derision—
Oh God, I'll have to work in television!

*(Everyone freezes, lights down on them, up on **CHRIS.**)*

CHRIS.

Well, thereby hangs a tale of tinseltown,
With all these people running up and down,
Things do look pretty stark. The lovebirds are—
What did he say?—

HAL.

So near and yet so far?

CHRIS.

Ah, yes. Then there's Jorjina and Alón.
Will they pull off what they've been called upon
To do? Will Agnes take the marriage veil,
Or will true love and common sense prevail?
And then there's our poor hero, my old friend,

His feet dug in, refusing to amend
His foolish dream. How will it all turn out?
Forgive us please, for leaving you in doubt,
If only for, say, fifteen minutes, but,
To quote the folks at Paramount...and cut!

    (blackout)

End of Act One

ACT TWO

Scene One

(ALÓN and JORJINA enter with their clapboards, come downstage center and claps as they did in Act I. they clap 3 times, then JORJINA takes ALÓN's and exits. The Masseur enters the scene. He lifts a cloth and ARNIE is discovered face down on a massage table. The Masseur works on him as ARNIE talks to himself. Words in caps indicate when the masseur is kneading him vigorously.)

ARNIE.

At every turn I'm met with sabotage,
Who cares? Some PT and a good MASSAGE,
A session with my therapist, some reike,
And I'm BACK to myself, no longer shaky
And vulnerable. Hah. I've been made the fool
By JERKFACE and a girl just out of school.
But I'm the very smartest GUY I know—
A self-made man, an impresario!
I've seen my friends get SCREWED all over town
But no one's gonna bring Phil Forrest DOWN!
Of course, there's always that first time you fail.
No, not if I take care of each detail,
Make sure my ASS is covered, just hang tough—
Produce it like a MOVIE—

(to the Masseur)

That's enough!

(He jumps off the table and exits to get dressed. The Masseur rolls the table off and makes a quick change into Pierre. **JORJINA** *and* **ALÓN** *enter.)*

ALÓN.

Jorjina!

JORJINA.

(entering, whispering)

What!?

ALÓN.

I can't go through with this!

JORJINA.

Of course you can. You got to. *Señor* Chris
Say it's the only way.

ALÓN.

He'll know it's me!

JORJINA.

He won't. He's so distracted, he can't see
The nose upon his face. Just go get dressed.

(seducing him again)

Enamorado...

(aside, as **ALÓN** *goes, reluctantly)*

He is very stressed!

CHRIS.

(entering)

All set?

JORJINA.

All set.

CHRIS.

The minute that it's done,
Come tell me.

JORJINA.

Oh, you bet.

CHRIS.

(aside)

Then starts the fun.

*(**ARNIE** enters, sees **CHRIS.**)*

ARNIE.

What do you want!!??

CHRIS.

*(signaling to **PIERRE**, who is in the house and enters the patio area)*

I'm back! And here's Pierre.

ARNIE.

Oh, God.

CHRIS.

What?

ARNIE.

Good.

(He opens the door to his neighbor's house.)

Go on, she's right up there.

CHRIS.

And here's the wardrobe, shoes, the ring, some flowers. When is the ceremony? Two, three hours?

ARNIE.

Fine.

*(**PIERRE** exits into the neighbor's house with the stuff. **ARNIE** is pacing)*

CHRIS.

Will there be a dinner?

ARNIE.

I can't eat.

CHRIS.

Ha! Wedding jitters! Doesn't that complete
The picture!?

ARNIE.

Your intense preoccupation
With other men's affairs is a vocation,
Isn't it?

CHRIS.

I learned the skill from you,
Old friend. What would you have me do?

ARNIE.

Butt out.

CHRIS.

Well, aren't we uptight tonight!
I would surmise that all is not quite right
With Agnes of the farm. I'd almost swear
That something's going on right up that stair.

ARNIE.

What makes you think that!?

CHRIS.

Call it intuition,
But your behavior fills me with suspicion.

ARNIE.

Ridiculous! There's nothing wrong at all.
I'm fine.

CHRIS.

I see that.

ARNIE.

Don't you have to call
That woman— ?

CHRIS.

Eve? She'll phone when she gets in.

ARNIE.

Well, go and get yourself some food!

CHRIS.

You win.

But I'm not leaving. Something is a-brewing,
And I am gonna find out what you're doing.

ARNIE.

You're such a character! Look, I'm right here,
You see me doing anything? It's clear
You've spent too much time at the movies. Now,
Why don't you go and fix yourself some chow?

> (CHRIS *exits as* JORJINA *enters— they give each other a look*)

JORJINA.

The judge, he call to say, no come, too busy,
He send another judge.

ARNIE.

All right, where is he?

JORJINA.

I go get him. I bring him here to you.
Now where he go? Señor, el judge, yoo hoo!

> (*She goes off and drags a reluctant* ALÓN *back in, very well disguised. He wears a robe and speaks with a different accent.*)

Oh, here he is, señor.

> (ALÓN *gives* JORJINA *a terrified look, then turns to* ARNIE. *Throughout the scene,* JORJINA *coaches* ALÓN *on what to say.*)

ALÓN.

Good evening, sir.

ARNIE.

> (*from this point on,* ARNIE *is completely distracted, unable to concentrate*)

I'm getting no support!

JORJINA.

You should confer
A few short minutes—

ARNIE.

Scripts! They're everywhere
Not one of them has got a plot to spare.
Stay calm, don't panic.

ALÓN.

Panic?!

JORJINA.

(to ALÓN)

Why should he?

(indicating a chair)

Sit down!

(She pushes him down at the table.)

ARNIE.

Can't let him get the best of me!

JORJINA.

No, no, senor, this judge, he very smart!
Tell him, your honor!

ALÓN.

Sí, I'm smart.

JORJINA.

Let's start.
A good idea, no? You must set up—

ARNIE.

I need a plan—

JORJINA.

You need a good pre-nup.

ALÓN.

Sí! All your property will be at stake—

ARNIE.

I must be careful—

ALÓN.

How much did you make
Last year?

ARNIE.

How to protect my reputation?

JORJINA.

Let's put down six mil.

ALÓN.

(getting more confidence)

That's a good foundation—

ARNIE.

— And keep the press away—

ALÓN.

Perhaps creation

Of a trust? To add to the equation—

ARNIE.

And keep her happy—

JORJINA.

With one complication.

You have to put clause 5 in a rotation

With 41 sub-A—Avoid taxation

Of the trust—

ARNIE.

I love her.

ALÓN.

Then conciliation

Will be yours.

ARNIE.

I love her.

JORJINA.

If inflation

Is a problem, then a delegation

Of a P of A—

ARNIE.

I love her!

ALÓN.
Preservation

Of the principal—

ARNIE.

I—

ALÓN.
Prefixation

Of the interest—

ARNIE.

Love—

JORJINA.
Adjudication

Of the profit—

ARNIE.

That—

ALÓN.
If procreation

Is a factor—

ARNIE.

Girl!

ALÓN.
Then application

Of a dividend, or mediation
As a last resort, if you prefer.
And that should do it.

JORJINA.
Nice work.

ARNIE.
I love her.

ALÓN.

(aside to JORJINA*)*

Here goes.

(to **ARNIE***)*

What is the name of this young bride?

ARNIE.

What? Agnes.

ALÓN.

Sir, the wedding's nullified
Unless I have her <u>last</u> name.

ARNIE.

I don't know.
I don't remember. It was long ago.
She was adopted...

ALÓN.

By?...

ARNIE.

Some family...

ALÓN.

The name?

ARNIE.

Is that important?

ALÓN.

Well, you see,
The problem is...the girl will be ex parte,
Without a last name.

ARNIE.

All right! It's... Duarte.

JORJINA.

Duarte.

ALÓN.

Thank you. That's it.

JORJINA.

Nice and clear.

ALÓN.

And watertight.

JORJINA.

Unsinkable.

ALÓN.

Sign here.

(**ALÓN** *puts the pen in* **ARNIE**'s *hand and moves it across the paper.*)

I'll take this back and write it up today.

ARNIE.

I love her. I can't let her get away!

(*He wanders around the side of the house.* **ALÓN** *removes the hairpiece and glasses and nose.*)

JORJINA.

We got it!

ALÓN.

Got it!

CHRIS.

(*entering*)

Got it?

ALÓN.

Got the name

CHRIS.

Good. Time for Uncle Juan to join the game.

(*He whips out his cell and dials as he exits;* **ALÓN** *and* **JORJINA** *exit opposite into the neighbor's house.*)

ARNIE.

(*aside, wandering back to the patio*)

OK. Now I can think what must be done
To see to it that putz is on the run
Within the hour. He must not get by
Jorjina and Alón again. He'll try,
He's got that thousand, and they can be bought.

(*looks at his reflection in the window*)

Just perfect. Are you happy, you big shot?
You're in too deep to back out now, you're stuck.
If this blows up you'll be a sitting duck
For all those other schmucks you ridiculed.
You can't hide from those guys—they won't be fooled.

(He goes to the neighbor's house and calls:)

Alón! Jorjina!

ALÓN & JORJINA.

(entering)

Here we come again!

ALÓN.

You catch the guy, *señor?*

ARNIE.

Almost!

JORJINA.

Muy bien!

ARNIE.

But he is devious.

ALÓN.

Oh.

ARNIE.

You don't know when
He'll come around and offer you a bribe.

JORJINA.

What's that?

ARNIE.

A very bad thing. I'll describe.
I'll be the young man.

ALÓN.

You.

ARNIE.

And you'll be you.

ALÓN & JORJINA.

Okay.

ARNIE.

Now, watch exactly what I do
And say.

ALÓN & JORJINA.

Okay.

ARNIE.

Alón, please help me!

ALÓN.

No!

ARNIE.

Jorjina, you are tenderhearted—

JORJINA.

Go!

ARNIE.

But I'm in pain!

JORJINA.

Too bad.

ARNIE.

My heart is broken!

ALÓN.

That's a shame.

JORJINA.

You must leave.

ALÓN.

We have spoken.

ARNIE.

All right. I understand. I'll leave right now.

JORJINA.

That's good.

ALÓN.

Goodbye.

ARNIE.

But if you would allow
A token of respect—

ALÓN.

What kind of token?

ARNIE.

A thousand dollars—

JORJINA.

Well, his heart is broken…

ALÓN.

Es verdad…

ARNIE.

It's just by way of thanks
For putting up with all my crazy pranks.

JORJINA.

That's reas'nable.

ARNIE.

The only thing I ask
Is just to let me see the girl. To bask
For one short moment more in her sweet light,
And then I'll disappear.

ALÓN.

Gone.

ARNIE.

Out of sight

For good.

ALÓN.

Jorjina, what you say?

JORJINA.

I say

No, sir. What you say?

ALÓN.

I say, no way!

JORJINA.

¡Hijo de puta!

ALÓN.

You a nasty boy.

JORJINA.

You want *la señorita* to destroy
The marriage plans of *El Señor?*

ALÓN.

That's bad.

JORJINA.

You and *la señorita* should be glad
A nice rich man like *el señor* desire
To marry her and baby, light her fire.
So what if she so young and he so old?
The fire in his veins a little cold—

ALÓN.

You must remember, he got lots of money!
What can you give her? Love?

JORJINA.

That's very funny.

ARNIE.

I—

ALÓN.

All the people here in Hollywood,
They very, very smart. They know what's good
For you—

JORJINA.

And me—

ALÓN.

And young girls like Agnès.
Already that old man, he buy a dress
For her! So even though she cry and cry
For you, you got to say adios.

JORJINA.

Bye bye.
Just take your heart and smash it with your hand.

ALÓN.

There's no place for true love in Lalaland.

JORJINA.

That's what we say when that man come once more.

(With the hundred bucks, they go to the door and open it.)

ALÓN.

We just say no!

JORJINA.

And then we slam the door!

(They slam it, exiting.)

ARNIE.

(aside)

I'm glad I hired them. They had potential.
I saw it right away. It is essential
To have support around you, who can smash
The opposition and— they took the CASH!
I bet they're in collusion with that kid!
And Agnes too! All right, time to get rid
Of everybody standing in my way!
At this point, I say murder is fair play!

(Over old time movie music and strobe lights, ARNIE rushes over and opens the neighbor's door. The façade of the house swings open to reveal AGNES' room, which has a window, a double closet door and a door to the bathroom). ARNIE climbs the stairs behind the façade as HAL climbs in the window and kisses AGNES. In the middle of the kiss, they separate—a footstep on the stairs! HAL dives into the closet as JORJINA and ALÓN burst in the room and point to the hallway and stairs. ALÓN dives into the closet as well. JORJINA stands by AGNES, as ARNIE enters. He tears around the room, looks under the bed, under a dressing table skirt, then opens the left closet door, revealing ALÓN standing there. He puts the

one thousand dollars in **ARNIE***'s hand.* **ARNIE** *slams the door, starts to leave, turns around, opens the other side of the closet and* **ALÓN** *is standing there. He closes the door, goes to the bathroom, opens the door and* **PIERRE** *is standing there, blow dryer aimed at* **ARNIE***, who jumps back in terror, thinking it's a gun aimed at him, grabs a can of hairspray and sprays* **PIERRE***'s face with it.* **PIERRE** *screams, grabs a towel and covers his eyes, running around the room.* **ARNIE** *leaves the room and starts back down the stairs.* **HAL** *emerges from the closet, bumps into* **PIERRE** *who ricochets back and falls out the window.* **ARNIE** *bursts back into the room as* **HAL** *jumps behind the door, which smashes into his nose and traps his hand.* **ARNIE** *looks around, closes the door and goes down the stairs.* **HAL***, nose and hand smashed by the door, stumbles out from behind the door, kisses* **AGNES** *on the cheek and dives out the window on top of* **PIERRE***. two screams of pain and—)*

(blackout)

Scene Two

(At lights up, **ARNIE** *is pacing, back in his own yard, some time later)*

ARNIE.

I'm sure he was up there! He's slippery!
I'll change the locks and keep the only key,
Put bars on all the windows.

HAL.

(Entering with a huge band aid on his nose to add to the bandage on his head. His hand is bandaged as well.)

Arnie!

ARNIE.

WHAT!?

HAL.

I'm so glad that you're still here. I cannot
Believe what's happening!

ARNIE.

Me too!

HAL.

The guy
Has turned into a loony tune!

ARNIE.

No! Why
Do you say that!?

HAL.

The last time I left you,
To go and figure out what I should do,
She came out on the balcony and waved.
I saw at once she wanted to be saved,
So risking everything I climbed the trellis.
If that old fart found out, would he be jealous!

ARNIE.

I bet he would.

HAL.

I made it to her room,
We kissed, aware of the impending doom,
The danger lurking near us everywhere,
Then, sudd'nly, thunderous footsteps on the stair!

ARNIE.

No!

HAL.

Yes! He had a bunch of thugs with him.
The thumping, coming toward us—

ARNIE.

Very grim.

HAL.

We stood there, frozen. It was scary—

ARNIE.

Was it?

HAL.

Then Agnes pushed me right into the closet!

ARNIE.

The closet!?

HAL.

That's right. I said I should stay
And face the dragon, but she said "no way,"
So in I went, right through the closet door—
Her dresses smelled so nice—two seconds more
And someone jumped right in beside me!

ARNIE.

Who?

HAL.

That guard. I was afraid what he might do,
So I grabbed him and said, "No funny stuff!"
I guess I let him know I could be tough,
So we just waited in there. Oh, the noise
When Forrest charged in there with all his boys—

ARNIE.

With all his boys?

HAL.

They tore around the place,

While Agnes screamed, sheer terror on her face—

ARNIE.

You saw her face!? And his!?

HAL.

Well, that's not true,

But there was just no telling what he'd do,

And then, when I thought I could stand no more,

The monster opened up the closet door!

ARNIE.

He did!?

HAL.

And there was no way I could run

And hide from him. I'm sure he pulled a gun,

Because Alón gave him his money. See

How horrible that slimy scum can be?

A thousand bucks that poor guy lost!

ARNIE.

How sad.

HAL.

The man's despicable!

ARNIE.

So very bad.

HAL.

You think we're dealing with a maniac?

ARNIE.

I do.

HAL.

Thank God I came through the attack.

ARNIE.

And you were in the closet?

HAL.

All the time.

He really scared my sweetheart.

ARNIE.

What a crime.

What happened then?

HAL.

Let's see...he went away.

I came out of the closet. Then halfway
Back down the stairs, he turned and barreled back!
I jumped behind the door, he opened smack
Into my face, as he took one more look.
I saw one of his henchmen, some poor shnook
Who, blinded by his boss, reeled round the room,
Then jumped out of the window to his doom!
I flew right out behind him, landed SPLAT
Right on that bruiser.

ARNIE.

Oh.

HAL.

And that was that.

I think he's at the hospital. Oh, sir,
This guy's a nut case. I'm afraid for her.
We both decided we have had enough
And now it's time for us to both get tough.
We're leaving.

ARNIE.

Leaving!? Here?

HAL.

That's right—tonight!

And I am asking you to join the fight.

ALÓN.

You want my help!?

HAL.

I do, and desperately.
I'm coming back tonight to set her free,
And you could keep an eye on things for me
Down here, so I can help her down the ladder—
It gets dark early and— hey, what's the matter!?

ARNIE.

(gasping for air)

I can't—

HAL.

I've asked too much of you. Forgive
Me sir, I'm like a frightened fugitive.
I have no right to ask you to involve
Yourself. This problem must be mine to solve,
And I will do it, come what may. So long.
Just knowing you're with me makes me feel strong.

(he exits)

ARNIE.

Oh God, my heart! I cannot catch my breath!
My pulse, my lungs, I'm very close to death!

CHRIS.

(entering)

Well, don't you look a mess! What's going on?
Your hands are shaking, and your face is drawn…

ARNIE.

(Throughout the following scene with **CHRIS**, **ARNIE**
tries to get away but **CHRIS** *stops him.)*

The deal with Hanks fell through.

CHRIS.

Oh. Sorry, Phil.
It's only business, man, here—take a pill.

ARNIE.

Thanks.

CHRIS.

Now, my friend, we're gonna take a meeting.

ARNIE.

A meeting?

CHRIS.

Right. And there will be no cheating,
Hedging, double talking. You will put
All games aside and tell me what's afoot
With you and that sweet, simple, country lass.
Is it a go, or did she bust your ass?

ARNIE.

There are no busted asses anywhere
That I know of.

(*aside*)

Except perhaps Pierre.

CHRIS.

Well? Look, it's almost dark, so where's the wedding?

ARNIE.

A slight delay.

CHRIS.

Aha! Could we be heading
Toward disaster? Did she meet another guy?

ARNIE.

What!? Rumors!

CHRIS.

Really? Well, then, clarify.

ARNIE.

Whatever's going on, you can be sure
That Agnes of the farm is still as pure
As driven snow.

CHRIS.

Ah, yes, but who's the driver?

ARNIE.

Me! And if there were some cool conniver,
I'd find him out at once and shoot him down
Before I'd be abused all over town.

CHRIS.

Is that the test of your integrity?
Assurance of your wife's fidelity?

ARNIE.

You bet.

CHRIS.

That is some strange philosophy!
A man can lie and steal his way through life,
But if he has a faithful little wife
He's honorable?

ARNIE.

Yep.

CHRIS.

His reputation
Depends on someone else's assignation,
Although it's brief or meaningless?

ARNIE.

That's right.

CHRIS.

Pal, if your wife works up an appetite
For braving new horizons, why should you
Feel compromised for what she chose to do?
Who cares what others say?

ARNIE.

I do.

CHRIS.

Too bad.
Extremism could drive a fellow mad.

ARNIE.

I know.

CHRIS.

That's not to say we should declare
"My lovely wife is having an affair,
That's great!" but, Arnie, listen, this obsession
With purity is giving you depression,
Are you incapable of sitting back
And cutting her, to coin a phrase, some slack?
I'll tell you what, pal: do what I have done.
Light a cigar and say, "Go have some fun.
Oh yes, and one more little thing, my sweet,
Whatever your adventures, be discreet."

ARNIE.

You know, you're absolutely right.

CHRIS.

I am?

ARNIE.

You are. I've seen the light. It hit me, wham,
Between the eyes. I have too much at stake
To blow the marriage.

CHRIS.

True.

ARNIE.

I'm going to take
Your sound advice.

CHRIS.

You are?

ARNIE.

I mean it, Chris.

CHRIS.

Congratulations.

ARNIE.

On to wedded bliss.

(He tries to leave, **CHRIS** *stops him.)*

CHRIS.

And, if you find your wife's behavior crude,
And you can't change her, change your attitude.

ARNIE.

Hey, don't you have to go and pick up Eve?

CHRIS.

Right.

ARNIE.

Take the Jag again!

CHRIS.

Well, thanks.

ARNIE.

(aside, as he throws him the keys)

Just leave!

CHRIS.

I'll be right back.

ARNIE.

No hurry. Time enough.

(**CHRIS** *exits*)

Let's tear it up. Phil Forrest's getting tough!

(He goes to the neighbor's house and whispers:)

Alón? Jorjina?

ALÓN.

*(entering with **JORJINA** and whispering)*

Something wrong, señor?

ARNIE.

You bet there is. You're going off to war.

ALÓN.

We are?

JORJINA.

He is?

ARNIE.

Tonight.

JORJINA.

No!

ALÓN.

That's too soon.

ARNIE.

Don't worry. By tomorrow afternoon
You'll be discharged.

ALÓN.

That's fast. Who do we fight?

ARNIE.

The thief.

JORJINA.

The young man?

ARNIE.

He will come tonight
To steal my fiancée. And you and you
Are going to arrange a little coup.

JORJINA.

A coup?

ARNIE.

A coup. That's what you're going to do.
Tonight. You're going to hide.

ALÓN.

Where?

ARNIE.

Right outside
Her window. When he comes, you'll grab him quick,
Before he climbs the ladder. Then you'll stick
Him in the SUV.

ALÓN & JORJINA.

The SUV!?

ARNIE.

And get that creep as far away from me
And Agnes as you can. Right now! Go on!

JORJINA & ALÓN.

Where?

ARNIE.

Drive him all the way to Oregon!
I don't care! But remember, you can't tell
A soul what I just said.

ALÓN.

We go to hell
Before we rat on you.

JORJINA.

My tongue turn black
Before I say you started this attack—

ALÓN.

Stick needles in my eyes—

JORJINA.

Make me eat dirt—

ALÓN.

Slice me up good, until the blood she spurt—

JORJINA.

Pull out my fingernails—

ALÓN.

My toenails too—

JORJINA.

Beat me and choke me till my face turns blue—

ALÓN.

Cut off my ears—

JORJINA.

Torture me day and night—

ALÓN.

Stick spikes into my hands and feet—

ARNIE.

ALL RIGHT!!

Just go get rid of him.

JORJINA.

Oh, *sí, señor*!

We fix that guy!

(as they are leaving they say the next exchange)

ALÓN.

We pin him to the floor...

JORJINA.

And if he scream, we hit him in the head...

ALÓN.

We throw him down and kick him till he's dead...

JORJINA.

We push him off the cliff...

ALÓN.

Set him on fire...

JORJINA.

Soon he be singing with the angels' choir...

(And they're gone.)

ARNIE.

I'm justified. Call me tyrannical,

But this is no time to be merciful!

He's messing with my life. She can't think straight

Until I've given Mr. Stud the gate.

So watch out, kid, you're in my territory,

And you know I make movies dark and gory!

*(Music. The lights dim as **ARNIE** pours himself another drink and waits. Slow blackout except for lights behind **AGNES**' window. Silent movie again. **ARNIE** hides upstage behind a potted plant. The ladder goes up, **AGNES** comes out on the balcony, reaches out her arms, then a body falls from above and the ladder crashes to the*

ground. A thud, a groan, and **AGNES** *squeals, this time in fear.* **ARNIE** *comes out from behind the palm.)*

Can I produce a masterpiece or what?
That's all you need out here, a clever plot!

(He goes to the fence and looks over into the neighbor's yard.)

You don't suppose they meant that stuff about
The cliff...the fire...what if they took him out?
He might be hurt. It's possible he's...dead.
Oh no, I must have been out of my head!
It sounded like things got way out of hand,
But surely the police will understand?
A crime of passion? No, I'll have to blame
Jorjina and Alón. Must keep my name
Way out of this. Oh God, what have I done!?
Now I'm a movie mogul on the run!
I'll take the Jag and drive right off the hills—
No, turn the gas on, swallow all my pills,
Walk in the ocean, just like Norman Maine,
No wait! There must be some way to explain—
I thought it was a burglar—yes, of course!
He climbed a ladder and he tried to force
Himself upon my dearest fiancée,
No, she's in shock, can't talk right now, I'll say—
No, don't say anything, that's how to play—

*(**HAL** has entered and stands behind **ARNIE**, wearing a head bandage and knee brace and limping. **ARNIE** turns around suddenly and sees him.)*

Aarrgghh!

HAL.

Aarrgghh! What's wrong!?

ARNIE.

Are you okay?

HAL.

Yes!

ARNIE.

Yes!?

(aside)

Oh, thank you God.

HAL.

Although you'll never guess
What happened with my latest rescue plan
To save poor Agnes from that awful man.

ARNIE.

Oh, what the hell, let's hear it. Dazzle me.

HAL.

Well, there I was—

ARNIE.

Where?

HAL.

Hidden in that tree
Outside her window, crouching on my knees
For hours, it seemed. I prayed to heaven, please
Deliver Agnes safely unto me.
I waited, it got dark, I couldn't see—

ARNIE.

And then?

HAL.

I made my move. And this is dumb—
From crouching all those hours, my legs were numb.
I stood, to push the ladder into place,
My legs gave way, I tumbled into space
And BAM! I hit the ground and smacked my head.
I passed out. Agnes thought that I was dead.

ARNIE.

But here you are, and in one piece.

HAL.

I'm blessed.

God's on our side.

ARNIE.

I noticed. What's the rest?

HAL.

Well, there I was, out cold and on the ground.
The next thing I remember was the sound
Of someone whispering right in my ear.
"Don't worry, darling boy, Agnes is here,
I'll never leave you, ever."

ARNIE.

She said that?

HAL.

She did. And then she swore to me out flat,
"I will not go back in that house again.
I'm through with that old man." Amen.

ARNIE.

Amen.

HAL.

How brave she was for all her innocence.
She asked me if I'd come to her defense
If the old fart put up a fight. Of course,
I said "of course." But to enforce
A plan of action I need your assistance.

ARNIE.

I can't—

HAL.

Oh, don't say no, sir, our existence
Depends upon you!

ARNIE.

If I only could,
I'd do whatever—

HAL.

Yes, you've been so good,
Don't fail us now.

ARNIE.

But son, my neighbor is
A friend of mine. We're colleagues in the biz.
He could make trouble if he knew that I
Had interfered.

HAL.

We'd never tell! We'd die
Before we'd blab.

ARNIE.

Too risky—

HAL.

All we need
Is some place safe for her to hide—

ARNIE.

Agreed.

HAL.

It's such an imposition—

ARNIE.

Not at all.

HAL.

As you can tell, we're up against a wall—

ARNIE.

I'll take her!

HAL.

If I didn't love her so,
I'd never ask you.

ARNIE.

Okay!!

HAL.

As you know,
I love her more than words could ever say.

                    ARNIE.

No need to try—

                    HAL.

        We'll have to run away—

                    ARNIE.

How soon!?

                    HAL.

        A day or two—

                    ARNIE.

            Bring her to me.

I'll keep her here in total secrecy.

                    HAL.

My father will resist. He sent a fax,

Demanding that I meet him.

                    ARNIE.

            Just relax—

                    HAL.

I wonder what he wants—

                    ARNIE.

            No need to worry

Over him. Let's go and get her—HURRY!

                    HAL.

My gratitude is boundless—

                    ARNIE.

                Very nice.

                    HAL.

I'm just so grateful—

                    ARNIE.

            Yes, you've said that twice.

Where is she!!??

                    HAL.

            Down the street, behind a tree.

She's in disguise.

ARNIE.

Fine. Bring her here to me.

HAL.

You should disguise yourself as well. Protection.
Here. I brought three of these—

(He takes out two pairs of sunglasses and two hats, wigs {designer's choice}, gives one disguise to **ARNIE** *and puts the other on himself.* **ARNIE** *dons the disguise and starts off stage after* **AGNES.***)*

No! wrong direction!
She's this way!

ARNIE.

Oh.

HAL.

You wait here. I will bring
Her here. And thanks a million.

(He exits.)

ARNIE.

(aside)

I could sing
For joy the way this deal is working out!
Once I've got her alone, without a doubt
She'll see the difference between us two
The puppy and the warrior. Adieu,
You poor excuse for manhood! Catch you later!
You just got offed by me—the Terminator!

*(**HAL** re-enters with a reluctant **AGNES.**)*

AGNES.

Oh, please don't leave me!

HAL.

Dearest love, it's just
A little while. Two days tops.

AGNES.

No!

HAL.

You must.

This man knows everything we've done.

AGNES.

But who—

HAL.

My father's friend. He'll take good care of you.

AGNES.

I'm scared.

HAL.

Don't be. I'm yours, and you are mine.

I promise everything will turn out fine.

(He looks around, takes off his and her nose/glasses disguise, kisses her, puts them back on and exits.).

ARNIE.

(disguising his voice)

You're safe with me.

AGNES.

Oh, thank you, kindly, sir.

ARNIE.

I'm glad to be of help. Who would deter

The plans of two young lovebirds?

AGNES.

He would.

ARNIE.

Who?

AGNES.

A man I know. He'd kill you if he knew

You were protecting me—

ARNIE.

As bad as that?

AGNES.

Much worse!

ARNIE.

Well, don't you worry, pussycat,

I'll—

AGNES.

Whud you say?

ARNIE.

Me? Not a thing.

AGNES.

(pulling off his disguise)

You traitor!

You deceived us both!

ARNIE.

My love is greater

Than my promise to that stupid kid.

AGNES.

You killed my love for you—that's what you did!

Oh, Hal, where are you!?

ARNIE.

Go ahead and yell,

He's left you here with me, in a nutshell,

So I can see your lovely innocence

In all its glory. Drop the sweet pretense,

I don't believe it any more. Naïve!?

Of course, until you're ready to deceive

The man who took you out of the pig pen,

Who gave you such advantages, and then

Bestowed on you the honor of his love,

Asked only that you place his needs above

All others, and what do you do? You run

Into the arms of some young punk. You shun

The kindness I have shown you all these years

For carnal passion with a stud! Three cheers
For your upbringing! I'll be called the fool
By everyone. By God, I'll sue that school!
A stupid girl turns out to be a smarty—
It's comical—I ought to throw a party!
You've loved me nearly all your simple life,
Why wouldn't you be THRILLED TO BE MY WIFE?!!

AGNES.

Stop shouting, please! You're scaring me!

ARNIE.

You!? Scared?
Don't make me laugh. Here you are, all prepared
To go to hell for your debauchery.

AGNES.

Debauchery!? He wants to marry me!
You said yourself, it's not a sin if I'm
The wife of my true love. So where's the crime!?

ARNIE.

The crime is being his wife and not mine!
I mean for us to marry, so resign
Yourself—

AGNES.

No! he's the one who makes me tingle.
When you hug me I never feel a single
Tingle. I don't feel a thing with you.

ARNIE.

A tingle!? Oh, my dear, don't misconstrue
A tingle for true love. They're not the same.

AGNES.

They are for me. I love him. He's a flame
That lights me up inside. I don't know why
It should be like that—

ARNIE.

No?

AGNES.

I didn't try
To make it happen. It just did.

ARNIE.

Your soul,
My little one, could exercise control
And concentrate on he who loves you best,
Who's loved you best for years—

AGNES.

Give it a rest!

I don't love you.

ARNIE.

You don't?

AGNES.

No.

ARNIE.

No?

AGNES.

No.

ARNIE.

So.

Why not?

AGNES.

Why not!?

ARNIE.

I have a right to know.

AGNES.

Because I love Hal!

ARNIE.

Two days and you're sure?

AGNES.

I know it in my heart.

ARNIE.

Love can't endure
Unless you know the guy for years and years.

AGNES.

Like you knew me.

ARNIE.

Exactly. It appears

As friendship first, establishment of trust,

Affinity which then starts to adjust

Itself into a deeper, richer feeling.

Before you know it, Agnes dear, you're squealing.

> *(He kisses her, long and tenderly. She gives a pathetic little squeal.)*

AGNES.

I'm sorry, Uncle Phil, it's just not there.

When I'm around you, it's not anywhere.

When I'm with Hal, it fills me to the brim.

He loves me, Uncle Phil, and I love him.

ARNIE.

I tried to bring you up so carefully!

You think I did all that to set you free?

AGNES.

You tried to bring me up so I would be

Naive, uncultured, unsophisticated.

I'm like some doll you think you have created

To fall in love the minute you play Cupid.

Why should I love a man who thinks I'm stupid?

ARNIE.

And what about the money I have spent!?

AGNES.

Each dollar, dime and nickel, every cent

Will be returned to you by Hal and me,

If I must work until I'm ninety-three—

ARNIE.

It's not the money! I want you, my sweet.

Look, let's stop fighting. We'll make a complete

New start to everything. You'll come and go
Whenever you desire. A new trousseau,
A trip to Maui, Paris, shopping sprees,
A Beemer and a driver. Let me please
My little princess. Why are you so quiet?
You can't know if you'll like it till you try it.
No wait, don't answer yet. Perhaps I spoke
Too hastily. Here, take another Coke,
Go in the guest house, just a little while,
And think it over. And let's have a smile,
A little tiny one? For Uncle Phil?
You'll make the best choice—I just know you will.

> *(He walks her off left, we hear a door slam and a key
> turn. He returns.)*

What has become of me? That boy was right!
I've turned into a loony in one night!
Well, I can't help it. I have been betrayed
And I must see the end of this charade.
I'm keeping her locked up, and I don't care
If all of Hollywood knows she's in there!

> *(He exits. Over music, **JORJINA** enters, talking on a cell
> phone. Periodically we hear **AGNES**' muffled voice and
> some pounding. **HAL** enters, talking wildly on his cell
> phone, exits again, Pierre, in a leg cast and on a crutch
> hobbles through and goes back into the neighbor's house.
> **ARNIE** comes back, lights come up as **HAL** re-enters.)*

HAL.

Oh, sir, you'll never guess!

ARNIE.

All right, I'll bite.

HAL.

My father's on his way here!

ARNIE.

Now? Tonight!?

How do you know?

HAL.

He called me on the cell!
He's turned my life into a living hell.
He said I absolutely can't elope
With anybody! But, I couldn't cope
If I lost his affection! But my love!

ARNIE.

A sticky situation.

HAL.

Gods above!
I don't know why young people have to suffer
For their love.

ARNIE.

Sad.

HAL.

You could be a buffer
To his anger—

ARNIE.

Well—

HAL.

You're his best friend!
He'd listen to you!

ARNIE.

(aside)

Does this never end?

(to him)

So you want me to speak on your behalf.

HAL.

Oh, would you?

ARNIE.

(aside)

This might be good for a laugh.

(to him)

What should I say?

HAL.

That Agnes is a prize
To be sought after. And you would advise
That he give us his blessing.

ARNIE.

Blessing.

HAL.

Yes!

Make sure he knows we both want him to bless
Our marriage.

ARNIE.

Ah.

HAL.

You know he can be strict—

ARNIE.

Oh yes, indeed—

HAL.

If he thinks I have picked
A girl to marry that he hasn't seen,
And with no fam'ly—

ARNIE.

I see what you mean.
I'll speak to him the minute he gets here.

HAL.

Oh thank you!

ARNIE.

I will make it crystal clear
What I think you, the loyal son, should do.

HAL.

We owe our future happiness to you.
But where is Agnes?

ARNIE.

Safely locked away.

(aside)

This is the climax. This is where you pay,
And get to watch my new special effects.

CHRIS.

(bursting in with **RON** *and* **EVE** *)*

Look who I ran into at L.A.X.!

RON.

(rushing over and embracing **ARNIE** *)*

You hound dog!

ARNIE.

Ron! Just look at you, old fart!

RON.

You relic.

ARNIE.

All these years we've been apart—

RON.

Thank God for friends like you.

ARNIE.

No, friends like you.

CHRIS.

And this is Eve!

ARNIE.

Hello.

EVE.

How do you do.

AGNES.

(offstage and muffled until she enters)

Yoo hoo?

HAL.

Who's that?

> ARNIE.

Who's what?

> AGNES.

I can't get out!

> ARNIE.

LET'S ALL GO IN THE HOUSE!

> CHRIS.

No need to shout.

> ARNIE.

AND HERE'S YOUR BOY!

> RON.

(crossing to him and looking at all the bandages and leg brace)

What happened? You're a mess!

Is this about that girl?

> HAL.

Well, I—

> RON.

Confess!

> HAL.

You don't know the whole story.

> RON.

No, I don't,

And I don't want to.

> HAL.

Listen Dad—

> RON.

I won't.

> HAL.

(to ARNIE*)*

Now, Arnie, please!

> ARNIE.

Right.

(to **RON***)*

>   What's the buzz, old friend?

RON.

He's met some fortune hunter.

(to **HAL***)*

>   Don't pretend

She isn't.

HAL.

  Sir?

ARNIE.

>   So, Ron, you don't approve?

RON.

Of course not.

ARNIE.

>   And you'd like her to remove
Herself at once from your son's premises?

RON.

Exactly.

ARNIE.

>   And a son should always please
His father. Who has worked hard to provide
A good life for his child.

HAL.

>   Huh?—

ARNIE.

>   Been a guide,
Directing him from infant to adult—

RON.

Right on.

ARNIE.

>   Raising a child is difficult—

HAL.

What's going on!?

AGNES.

Help?

ARNIE.

HELP! Is what you give

When you want to ensure your son will live

A better life than you had.

RON.

Nicely put.

ARNIE.

(stomping his foot to hide **AGNES**'s *thumping on the door)*

There are those times when down must come the foot,

To make sure that a very grave mistake

Will not be made. This is the time to take

A good long look at what is best for him.

RON.

So true.

HAL.

WAIT!

ARNIE.

There could be some grim

Results if you do not take a firm hand—

AGNES.

I'm locked in!

ARNIE.

LOCKED IN! Sinking in quicksand,

Is how he could end up—a life of strife,

And all because he married the wrong wife.

HAL.

Why have you turned on us!?

RON.

Hal! Shame on you!

He only wants to help you!

HAL.

That's not true!

You liar!

ARNIE.

Easy, lad.

RON.

Apologize!

HAL.

I won't!

ARNIE.

It's OK.

RON.

No! No compromise
On this. You treat your elders with respect!
It's that girl's fault, just look at the effect
She's had on you!

HAL.

You said you'd help!

ARNIE.

I said
I'd talk to him. And now I have.

HAL.

I'm dead.

EVE.

Excuse me, Ron.

RON.

What?

EVE.

Do you love your son?

RON.

Of course. That should be clear to everyone.

EVE.

I'm sure it is. You want his happiness.

RON.

Yes, but—

EVE.

But he stands here, in real distress
Because you won't consent to even meet
A girl he thinks will make his life complete.
She may not be a fortune hunter.

RON.

No?

EVE.

Perhaps she's Juliet to his Romeo.

HAL.

Oh yeah, she is!

RON.

Do you have children?

CHRIS.

Yes.

EVE.

No.

CHRIS.

Yes.

RON.

Which is it?

EVE.

We should not digress
From this young man's dilemma.

   (to **HAL***)*

Where is she?

HAL.

Where is she?

   (There is a thud, as if someone had run at a door and thrown herself at it, followed by a muffled "OW!")

   Agnes!

AGNES.

Help!

HAL.

I'm here! Stand clear!

I'm breaking down the door!

(Everyone parts as **HAL** *runs offstage in the direction* **ARNIE** *took* **AGNES**. *We hear a thud, a crack of wood, another "OW!" and the two of them limp back on holding each other up and rubbing their shoulders.)*

AGNES.

Oh, Uncle Phil!

How could you!

HAL.

Uncle Phil!?

ARNIE.

I think I'm ill.

RON.

This is the girl?

HAL.

Yes.

RON.

She belongs to you?

ARNIE.

Yes.

AGNES.

No!

ARNIE.

I raised you, didn't I?

AGNES.

Not true!

He locked me in a school, where I was trained,

Like someone's dog, to grow up featherbrained.

ARNIE.

I paid for every stitch upon her back.

Saw to it there was nothing she might lack,

And now she wants to run away from me.

RON.

With my son.

ARNIE.

Who she's known two days.

EVE.

I see.

It's very hard to lose one's child.

ARNIE.

That's right!

A caring guardian should put up a fight.

What would you do?

EVE.

I'm not sure. Let me say,

If I could find my child, I'd find a way

To make her happiness my first concern.

RON.

You lost your child?

CHRIS.

She did, but she'll soon learn

Her whereabouts.

EVE.

It's why I came to town.

Chris said some fellow might have tracked her down.

ALL.

Oh!

EVE.

But I'm sure he is mistaken.

ALL.

Oh.

JORJINA.

How did you lose her?

EVE.

It was long ago.
A very common story. I was young,
In love, of course. But Fate was cruel and flung
Me to the winds. The boy was free and wild,
He loved me, then he left me with a child.
To keep her at the time was not an option.

ALL.

Awww.

EVE.

So, I had no recourse but adoption.
Through friends I gave her to a family
Up north.

JORJINA.

But who?

CHRIS.

And there's the mystery.
They changed their name and hers.

ALL.

Ooh.

CHRIS.

Years went by,
And fin'ly I've persuaded her to try
To find the child she lost so tragically.

ALL.

AH!

EVE.

But the Fates still act with treachery.
I've talked with lawyers, hired a detective,
But all their searches have been ineffective.
I came here to explore this one more lead,
But as things stand I doubt we will succeed.

CHRIS.

You WILL.

EVE.

Oh Chris, you know the lawyer says no.

JORJINA.

(knowing full well the answer)

Where did you leave her?

EVE.

On a farm near Fresno.

ARNIE.

A raisin farm?

EVE.

Why, yes, how did you know?

CHRIS.

Now this would be the moment for slo-mo.

(And it is.)

EVE.

I've prayed for years that we would find each other.
To come so close and then to lose it—

AGNES.

MOTHER!!!

(She flings herself—slomo— into EVE's arms)

ARNIE.

Oh no!

RON.

My God!

CHRIS.

Well, I'll be— .!

EVE.

You!?

AGNES.

Yes!

ARNIE.

But—

EVE.

My dearest child!

AGNES.

My mother?

JORJINA & ALÓN.

Sí!

CHRIS.

And cut.

HAL.

Dad? This is Agnes. Agnes, meet my dad!

RON.

Well, well. Hello, my dear.

AGNES.

I'm very glad

To meet you, sir. This is my mother.

RON.

Yes,

We've met.

EVE.

I'm mystified, I must confess.

How did this happen?

ARNIE.

How did I get screwed?

HAL.

You lied to me and everybody, dude.

RON.

But how—

EVE.

Chris said to come here right away.

CHRIS.

I knew that there was no time to delay.

EVE.

And then there was a phone call.

JORJINA & ALÓN.

Uncle Juan.

EVE.

Yes, that's his name! He told me he had gone
To Fresno to explore a lead—

ARNIE.

The name!

The judge!

(looking around at everybody, settling on **ALÓN***)*

How did you get into the game?

ALÓN.

We do what *Señor* Chris tell us to do.

ARNIE.

Now wait a minute! I owe this to you!?

CHRIS.

I had to set up something quick, my friend,
Since you seemed so unwilling to unbend.
The game was making sure you didn't make
A huge mistake. For yours and Agnes' sake.

ARNIE.

I see what this is. A conspiracy
To take my fiancée away from me!
You're in on it together! All of you!
Well, I'll just have to do what I must do.
I'm still the legal guardian and I say
She isn't getting married. Not today,
Not any day, not to this Romeo!

CHRIS.

(to everyone)

Excuse us please.

(He takes **ARNIE** *aside.)*

You've got to let it go,
Old pal. You said yourself you were concerned
About the rumors. So far, you're not burned,
Nobody knows outside of this small group.
Just cut your losses and you'll soon recoup
Your dignity. Let Agnes have her Juvey.

ARNIE.

Humiliating.

CHRIS.

Nah. Just make the movie.
You've got a plot, good characters, you are
Ahead already.

ARNIE.

What about the star?

CHRIS.

Get Ford. Dinero! Hoffman? Affleck?

ARNIE.

Wait!

DiCaprio!

CHRIS.

You're twenty years too late.

(turning to everyone)

I think we're going to work this out, my friends,
With lots of benefits and dividends
For everyone.

AGNES.

Hal!

HAL.

Agnes!

EVE.

Daughter!

RON.

Son!

CHRIS.

I'd say it was high time we had some fun.

(HAL and AGNES start into the house. ARNIE stands miserably to one side, watching his dream walk away with the "Juvey." CHRIS looks at him and EVE for a moment, then walks by ARNIE and "accidentally" shoves him closer to her, then moves upstage as they look at each other)

EVE.

I like your movies.

ARNIE.

Really? Thanks a lot.

Let's go inside—I'll show you one.

EVE.

Why not?

CHRIS.

(aside, as they cross into the house)

What's this? A hero's transformation?

ARNIE.

(with skepticism)

Maybe.

CHRIS.

Let's celebrate!

(Lots of chattering and noise, as everyone exits but ALÓN and JORJINA.)

ALÓN & JORJINA.

Hasta la vista— baby!

(From offstage, we hear music from The Terminator, *a voice calls "Cut! It's a wrap!" The movie set lights go off and the stage goes to black—)*

(blackout)

The End

www.ingramcontent.com/pod-product-compliance
Lightning Source LLC
Chambersburg PA
CBHW070326120726
47909CB00008B/2609